Sentiment

Vincent O'Sullivan

Solis Press

ALSO BY VINCENT O'SULLIVAN AND AVAILABLE FROM SOLIS PRESS:

The Good Girl
A Book of Bargains
Sentiment and Other Stories

Publisher's note: This version of *Sentiment* is very similar to that published in the 1914 book *Sentiment and Other Stories* (which is also available from Solis Press). Significant differences are that the author added references to the First World War and a final chapter to this later version of the story.

Originally published in 1917 by Small, Maynard & Company, Boston, USA and contains words that may offend. This edition completely reset with minor spelling changes and published in 2015 by Solis Press

ISBN: 978-1-910146-15-6

Published by Solis Press, PO Box 482,
Tunbridge Wells TN2 9QT, Kent, England

Web: www.solispress.com | *Twitter*: @SolisPress

CONTENTS

The Good Girl

A novel of permanent literary significance which, says Mr. Edward Garnett in the *Atlantic Monthly*, "entitles its author to a place among the first twenty American novelists."

"It is a work of genius in every sense of that word," says Mr. John Cowper Powys in his *One Hundred Best Books*, "and it produces on the mind that curious sense of completeness and finality which only such works produce."

"It does what I have always desired should be done," says Mr. L. U. Wilkinson: "it reduces atmosphere and nature to their proper subordinate places. It wastes no energy. It focuses one's intellect and one's emotion. It creates characters who resemble no others in fiction. It is imaginative realism of the highest level of excellence."

"It is not too much to say that *The Good Girl* is one of the twenty best books by living American novelists."—*New York Evening Post*.

"Its exceptional interest and quality," says Mr. J. B. Kerfoot in *Life*, "are hereby commended to lovers of good fiction."

Royal 8vo.   Paper/ebooks.   250 pages.

The First Part

"Oh, but that doesn't prevent sentiment."   Mallarmé

Chapter I

WILLIAM TORE ALONG THE platform of the suburban station with a newspaper streaming in his hand, while angry or encouraging shouts were hurled at him from several points by officials; bounded upon the step of the slowly moving train; and was pitched forward into the carriage by a brace of porters who stood ready. The door was slammed; William picked himself off the knees and toes of the other passengers, and gathered his hat from the floor at the far end of the carriage where it had rebounded from the nose of a lady in the corner. Then he sat down, opened his newspaper, and glancing round on faces flushed with pain and indignation: "That was a close shave," he observed genially.

His companions could not trust themselves to reply, and habit had inured William not to expect one unless it came in the form of sarcasm or vituperation. He had never yet met the passenger who smiled amiably on his descent, and was thereupon prepared to engage in a sparkling conversation. Indeed, he was now so experienced that he could derive the social order of his companions from their mode of receiving him. The genteel, he found, eyed him with silent fury, moving as they did in circles where a look is considered enough; but as you went down the ladder you encountered irony and objurgation. "Bloated aireoplane!" vociferated by a stout man, obviously a butcher, was the only fragment which had ever attracted more than the transient attention of William or lingered in his memory.

The scene, in fact, was repeated too often for him to class it any longer among his vivid excitements. This hare-brained rush and plunge took place about four times a week, and had degenerated in the estimation of William from a sporting event to a form of exercise. With this in mind, he even so arranged matters as to arrive at the station when the train was starting. He needed to relax the muscles before settling himself to his desk in the offices of Messrs. Ibed Brothers and Co., the well-known importers of perfumes and chemicals in Frog Lane, of whose business he formed a not at all indispensable part.

He had entered this office when he was twenty; and although it was now some three years that he had been occupying a clerical stool more or less insecurely, still his post remained insignificant and his salary he thought derisory. If his mother, a lady who supported existence at

Tunbridge Wells chiefly on a military pension bestowed upon her as the widow of Lieutenant-Colonel Spring, D.S.O., had not sent him occasional contributions, he would have found life in London, which he regarded with the same eye as the redoubtable Corinthian Tom, a grey and hopeless affair. To sit at home at night he felt was paltry and even unmanly; the more obvious enjoyments of the town-dweller enticed him to the West End. There, by spending freely his own money, his mother's, and money of more ambiguous origin in the gilded haunts of pleasure, he acquired enough of the gilt to cover any stains left by the office.

For the clerks to receive private correspondence addressed to the care of the firm was an act discouraged at Ibed Brothers, the firm having deduced from its experience that such missives went to furthering amatory and other intrigues which it was desirable to keep from the eye of the home circle. When, therefore, William, approaching his desk that Saturday morning, saw propped up an envelope addressed in an irregular but unmistakably female hand, he had a movement of impatience.

"That woman is a blighter! What does she want to write here for?"

The contents, however, were innocent enough. Stamped on top of the paper in small silver letters was the address of the writer: The Firs, Palebrook, Hampshire—and the letter meandered over the spacious page.

> July 3, 1914
>
> "DEAR WILLIAM,—I really can't think of your number, so write to the office, though your uncle says he thinks it's against the rules, but if it is you must see Mr. Ibed and explain it is a letter from your aunt and he is sure to be nice about it."

William paused, and reflected a moment gloomily on the character of women. "Now who with any sense would expect me to go into Ibed and say I had a letter from my aunt?" And he resumed his reading, with his opinion of the writer's knowledge of life, which had been small enough before, considerably lessened.

> "We want you to come down here just as soon as ever you get this and stay a month. Your vacation must be commencing, I should think, so you can easily manage it. It is long since you were here, not since you were quite a small boy, but you will not find us changed. I have written to your mother and told her you were going to spend your holidays with us.

Sabina Moll will be here part of the time. You remember Mr. Moll, don't you? We tried to get you into his office at Manchester before we arranged so well with Mr. Ibed. Give him my kindest regards. Your uncle sends his love, and I am your aff. aunt,

"LAURA S. M. BURGER.

"Mind you come *to-morrow (Saturday)* for a month. I have *special* reasons."

Letters from his aunt were by no means frequent enough to have laid the spirit of criticism. "Except for a Christmas card, price twopence, this is the first I've heard of her in near two years. I wonder what's up? 'Give him my kindest regards.' Oh, yes. Ibed doesn't care a rotten nut about her or about my uncle either. It wasn't them got me into the office; it was mother. They introduced mother to Ibed and she did the rest."

His thoughts lingered with a tenderness by no means usual upon the gay, still handsome widow at Tunbridge Wells, who took life so airily, whom nothing could mortify or depress. "Mother can do anything she likes," he reflected with a dash of bitterness. "With her looks and manner and way of jollying people along she could have married a millionaire before this. Why the devil hasn't she? That would have given me some chance, instead of being stuck in this dog-kennel which Aunt Laura is so proud to have found for me. I'll give Ibed her kindest regards, won't I? She must think I'm a kind of private secretary."

But all the same he was attracted by the invitation. He remembered Aunt Laura's house at Palebrook and its comforts. The Burgers were very well off. A vacation spent with them would be a different business from and altogether more desirable than a slim top room in his mother's boarding-house, dodging bored and aimless about the Pantiles, and smoking too much. Oh, yes, he would certainly put in a month with the Burgers.

But could he? Aunt Laura insisted upon his immediate appearance: the invitation seemed to depend on that. If he couldn't go now, perhaps he could not go at all. But the holidays at Ibed Brothers had not yet begun, and William's holiday lay far down the list near the last of August. He looked round upon his fellow-workers, meditatively gnawing a pen-handle.

"I'll go in and strike Ibed for an early vac.," he decided. "These fellows will be furious if I get it, but I don't care a horse-marine."

One of the partners, Mr. Behrens Ibed, had a fancy for dealing with the clerks personally. Was one to be rebuked or praised, his salary raised, or his name taken from the books, it was before Mr. Ibed, in person, that the patient plumed himself or wilted. And William, about an hour and a half later, found himself standing before a stout, good-humoured-looking, glossy little man, redolent, as it were, of his own perfumes. The black moustache spun out in points, the shining black hair which curled about the ears, the sallow complexion, were all but accessories to a pair of large lustrous brown eyes, laughing and jovial, though at certain moments they would suddenly turn hard and cold as an iceberg. But the prevailing expression was humour, even kindly humour; and in truth, whether Mr. Ibed was making a clerk happy by increasing his salary, or depriving a man of his livelihood, he liked to do it on a jest—though his jests often enough appealed to his listener much as judicial quips which set the court in a roar appeal to the prisoner in the dock.

"Well, Mr. Spring, what's gone wrong this morning?" He turned on William a face wreathed in smiles.

"I got a letter from my aunt——" William began awkwardly.

Mr. Ibed laughed sonorously. "Come, come, I'd no idea it was as bad as that. A letter from your aunt? Mr. Spring, this begins to look serious, sir. What does the lady accuse you of?"

With reservations, and a hashing of phrases, William shuffled through the facts and indicated his wishes.

"Hum! That's not so easy as you seem to think." Mr. Ibed looked hard at William, and something in the long-limbed, cool-faced young Saxon seemed to please him. "How's your mother?" he asked suddenly with decided interest.

"Oh, she's fairly well, I think," answered William gruffly. In secret he was flattered; but he always became gruff when he spoke of his family for fear that anybody should think he was carried away by inordinate affection.

"Fine woman, your mother," resumed the merchant with emphasis. "Right good sort, one of the best. You can tell her I said so. Well, look here, Mr. Spring—we stand to lose thousands by the loss of your services, but you can go."

William thanked him in the tone of one suffering from some indefinite sense of wrong, and slouched to the door.

"Oh, that's all right!" jocose Mr. Ibed fired a parting shot. "You can't enjoy yourself much if you think of those thousands your absence is going to cost us."

William approached Mr. Hamilton, the head clerk, a dour, iron-grey Scotsman. He tried to be airy, as though he were communicating a matter of infinitely little moment.

"Hullo, Mr. Hamilton, how's Scotland? By the way, I'm going for my holiday this afternoon. I've just seen the boss."

"Yill go one day and not be asked back, I'm thenkin'," said Hamilton, drawing down the corners of his mouth contemptuously into his beard. He seemed unmoved, but he eyed William with an unwonted glint of curiosity. A man who could have the date of his holiday advanced at Ibed Brothers must have some influence with the firm.

But the other clerks were by no means so self-contained. In fact, to most of these men, whose thoughts, however much they might hate the firm, necessarily centred on it as the chief interest of their existence, any variation of the rules had the effect of a revolution, and was a topic to be discussed for days. And the question of vacation, those few golden weeks of respite from the monotonous grind, was, together with the question of salary, the sorest question of all. William's companions were men of all ages, and most of the older ones suggested in some vague way that life had been too hard for them. You imagined, as you looked at them, the thousand lapses of dignity which an existence perforce genteel, that had to be kept up on inadequate means, had forced them into. But at this moment the eyes of all alike were lit by a similar flame of resentment and apprehension. Between the two main questions there was but a step, and one voiced the general fear.

"Have you got a rise?"

It was not that they had a corporate prejudice against William, or anything of that kind. Allowing for the peculiar conditions of the life of a clerk in a big firm, which tend to concentrate the thoughts of each individual on his private fortunes and to check any generous expansion towards his fellow-workers, it may be said that the young man was rather popular. True, he managed to irritate several of them on different sides by different traits. On many, his selfishness, disguised by no subtlety, but blatant and brutal as a schoolboy's, acted like the unexpected hoot of a motor-horn at a street corner. Then, the domineering and harsh manner which had not yet been worn down since his sojourn at Wellington College, a manner which often annoys men who have not been themselves at one of the big schools and consequently do not know what depth of uncertainty and shyness it covers, made against him here. There was no "give and take" about William at the office; he made no more effort to conciliate and win friends than the average sixth-form boy who is good at games. Besides, he was unmarried, and to many of these men, who came to their desks day after day weighted by domestic cares, he seemed to flaunt an insolent freedom for which they bore him a dull grudge, no less deep because it had no logical basis. And in truth, a man harassed with the baby's croup, or the incidents and expenses of his wife's lying-in, might be forgiven if he resented the sight of William's fresh-coloured, handsome face, self-satisfied and rather pompous, as he started on Saturday afternoon for cricket, tennis, or the river, without a serious trouble in the world. To make it worse, the young man was wont to relate his pleasures with a callousness and want of tact which proceeded partly no doubt from hide-bound indifference to the feelings of others, and partly from the obtuseness betokened by his good-looking headpiece.

For all that, he was well enough liked on the whole, and any ordinary performance of his would have roused no special indignation. But in the present matter he had clearly been hoisted over the heads of others—he, too, of all the clerks in the office the most incompetent. He was a creature of privilege, unjustly and arbitrarily conferred. For his sake, the scheme of holidays would have to be dislocated and new allocations made. Not an eye in the room but regarded him venomously. He, on his part, conscious that he was a target for obloquy, shoved things about on his desk with an elaborate assumption of unconcern.

"No," he answered the question. "I didn't get a rise, if you are anxious to know." Then, thinking this remark conciliatory to the point of cowardice, he added: "Of course I could have got it if I had liked. I'd only to ask."

This was brought out with such an accent of concealed power that for a moment his hearers were dumbfounded. Perhaps it might be as well not to rile such a manifest favourite of the Ibeds. And it really looked as if William was dominating the situation, when old Hamilton came in from another room. After a moment, he approached the young man's desk.

"Well, my laddie-buck," he said, addressing the favourite most dis-respectfully, "it'll be great pliskies you'll be havin' the night. And where do ye intend spendin' your holidays?"

The devil tempted William to swagger. "I'm going to stay at my aunt's place in Hampshire," he said incautiously.

The ears of the other clerks, stretched to preternatural keenness, caught the note of brag which sounded in this statement, and from that moment William was bombarded with his aunt. Was it his aunt who gave him his pretty ties and socks? Did his aunt take him out to walk on Sundays? Did his aunt tuck him up in bed at night?—Such were the inanities with which William was pelted. Descriptions of his aunt were built up with great skill, and every clerk lent his wit. One older, one at all events more philosophical, would have ignored them for their very vapidness; but William flushed and wriggled, his stony demeanour at last broken down. Silent and furious, he left the office as soon as he could, pursued with kind regards to his aunt, love to his aunt, kisses to his aunt. At the street door, the office-boy presented him with a letter and then fled. He opened it and found it was a proposal of marriage to his aunt.

"Lot of bounders!" he thought, as he flopped sulkily down on his seat in the train which bore him to his suburb. "They simply can't understand anything outside their own rotten kind of life."

This reflection restored in a measure his equanimity. It was not that he objected particularly to the gibes at his aunt for what they were worth; but it made him furious that anything connected with him, whether it were an aunt or a boot-jack, should be laughed at. He was in fact so unusually demoralized that he brought out his aunt's name at his lodgings with some embarrassment, and scanned his landlady's face suspiciously for the shadow of a smile. But the landlady received the address with so much satisfactory respect and even awe, that William had regained full possession of his self-esteem and his usual stock of assurance by the time he got on board the 3.15 from Waterloo.

As he sat, flanked by *Every Story has a Punch*, *Leggy Bits*, and other amusing publications, a thought flashed through his mind. "I ought to have gone round to see Penelope, I suppose. Forgot all about her. She's so infernally nervy. She'll make an awful row and love doing it." He yawned and stretched out his long legs. "Never mind; I'll write."

Now to this lady he was secretly engaged to be married.

Chapter II

Palebrook station lay rather outside of the town, and this had to be traversed before you reached "The Firs," which also lay a little outside the town at the far end. William, lounging back in the brougham which had been sent to meet him, stared vacantly out of the window. Some might perhaps have regarded with interest the singular winding little town, seated so picturesquely above the sea, a haven grey and salted from centuries of driving blasts and sea-mew, and now filled with the rumour of Saturday evening traffic; but William found difficulty in getting up an interest in anything where his own fortunes were not in some measure involved. He was thinking now of what kind of a month his aunt and uncle could manage to give him.

"I suppose the old lot are here in this hole just the same as when I was down ages ago. There'll be tennis, and croquet, and a few evening parties, when the natives are unselfish enough to sit up and give them. And cards. O Lord, how I loathe cards! I don't remember any decent girls when I was here last, but I was young then, I expect. Anyhow, it's better than Tunbridge Wells. I wish I was a millionaire."

This idle wish, probably the wish oftenest and most generally expressed throughout the civilized nations every twenty-four hours, ushered to his thoughts the name of Sabina Moll, for her father was rich. He fell to wondering what she would be like. Old Moll, the father, whom he had seen while he was still at school, he remembered as an infamous bore with a Lancashire accent, who asked puzzle questions in arithmetic and tipped badly. If Sabina was like her father, and Aunt Laura expected him to be nice to her, she would find herself jolly well mistaken, that's all! Even good-nature has its limit, and for William one aspect of that limit was the representation of old Moll as a female.

The carriage passed through a low iron gate painted red, and rolled over a short gravelled drive to the house. It was a fair-sized modern dwelling, standing amid trees, and surrounded by well-kept lawns and flower-beds. Had there been anything to complain of about the house, this might well have been overlooked on account of its pleasant seat. Perched on the crest of a hill, at its foot the salt marsh stretched level like a table, and above this the wild fowl swept in great companies. Where the line broke against the sky, you perceived from the windows the gleam of the torn breakers on the harbour-bar, while through the most lonely night you might always have the cheerful spectacle of the lights of ships riding at anchor. So, I say, might one have reasoned to whom the sights offered to the eyes were more important than comforts to lull the body; but, as it happened, it was unnecessary to discuss the alternative at "The Firs." Certainly, William, for one, would not have worn such an amiable smile as he entered the house if the aspect of it had not assured him of rewards other than good views from the windows.

His uncle stood in the hall and welcomed him with unfeigned heartiness; and his aunt pushed complaisance so far as to come out too, and seized him by both hands with manifest enjoyment. For a second, William feared that she was going to kiss him.

"They're uncommonly civil," he mused when he got to his room. "I wonder why they're so awfully glad to see me?"

His bedroom was a pattern of prettiness and comfort—of that English comfort which foreigners envy and strive after in vain. Even to William's unobservant eye, it was plain that Aunt Laura had taken special trouble to make things pleasant for him. Things done for him he generally took as if he expected they ought to be done; but in the flowers so deftly arranged, in the magazines lying about, and other trifles, he perceived an element of personal supervision which indicated that he was not only a nephew but a guest, and what was more, a guest they were anxious to please. He took up a book from the table by his bedside—the only book in the room—attracted by the heavy gilt binding, and put it down quickly in disgust. It was a gift to Aunt Laura, and *Indian Love Poems* was the title.

"What rot!" he commented. "If the Indians knew as much about love as I do they wouldn't write poetry about it. Why couldn't Aunt Laura stick some decent books around in case I got a reading fit?"

So, after all, he had discovered some kind of a grievance which saved him from any ridiculous lapse into gratitude. There was now no need to be expansive or to simulate the generous emotions; he was still free to face his relations from the advantageous standpoint of a person who has not been treated quite well. But as he worked through the long and perfectly cooked dinner, enhanced by full-bodied wines, and served, in a dining-room furnished in what seemed to him perfect taste, by two befrilled and noiseless maids, he found it hard to keep his injury in mind. Aunt and uncle, he found, were coming out strong, and he looked at them with a smile which was almost friendly. "If they keep this pace up for a month," he was thinking, "I shan't finish among the 'also ran.'"

"I've been looking at some of those papers you brought down," said his uncle. "We never get a glimpse of that kind of thing here. Quite spicy. Rather—rather—*French*, eh?"

"Tray French," answered William, whom the good cheer had gained to a reluctant kind of joviality.

"Throgmorton!" exclaimed Aunt Laura. When she used this name it was a sign that she was, or pretended to be, shocked, and her husband gave the chuckle of a sad dog in his plate. "I think," she went on smoothly in her rich melodious voice, "that one gets everything one wants in the sixpenny illustrated papers, don't you?" She turned to William. "And how was your mother looking when you saw her?"

"Ripping. Mother always looks well."

"Ah, there's a woman for you!" put in Mr. Burger. "None of your nonsense about *her*. What I call—I say, what *I* call a good specimen. Always laughing and in good humour. Wish we saw her here oftener, but she finds us too slow, I fancy. Now, I'm a kind of man who likes gaiety myself."

He was the husband of the sister—the much younger sister—of William's father, the deceased Lieutenant-Colonel, a detached position whence he could survey Mrs. Spring in untroubled lights, and admire what he called "the cut of her jib" without reserve. He did indeed like gaiety, as he said, and for years had yielded to this propensity in multifarious forms. Even still he had an occasional frisk, but he had long since laid aside the powdered gallantries of his youth. Fits of the gout, occurring with tedious periodicity, had warned him that tranquil courses were what he must for the most part follow in future if he would have peace. He recognized this mandate and acted upon it, though he would not acknowledge he did so to himself or anybody else. It is not so easy to cease to be a gay dog, and the reputation is clung to even after the substance is gone. Red-faced, pursy and active, nearer sixty than fifty, he expended his great fund of energy in tearing all over the country in a motor; in rough shooting; or again, the gulls might see him, drenched with spray, beating up the Solent in a small yacht. It is certain that he never gave a serious thought to anyone or anything but himself and his own concerns. Good luck had attended him through life—though you may well doubt this if you remember the terrible name "Throgmorton" which his wife had just now tossed at him. But as a matter of fact, his first name was Herbert, the auxiliary Throgmorton having been thrown in by his father as an act of grace, because (as Mr. Burger loved to relate) on the very day of his son's birth he had made a most lucky financial venture, engineered by a firm operating in Throgmorton Street, London. Lulled in comfort, he had no children to ruffle his equanimity, or distract attention from himself, and his slightest wish was anticipated by admirable servants. What more would you have? His conversation, which was listened to with respect by those who ate his excellent dinners, was as a rule the enunciation of weather-beaten commonplaces specialized to the individual. Most of us, so like one another, thinking ready-made thoughts, galvanizing stale emotions, sharing with my brother the cut of my coat and a parcel of opinions, with my sister her dressmaker and a bundle of phrases, as like, really, as one copy of the same newspaper is to another, into whatever odd shapes you may fold it; so few among us one, solitary, able to stand alone—well, most of us feel that a special god looks out of a special star concerned particularly with our own distinct being. Do many people really think that the world will go on *precisely* the same on the day after their death? And if you take a man who is the head or centrepiece, whether of a family in a cottage, or a court in a palace, feared, if not respected, consulted in all exigencies, it will go hard but he will think his opinions as important to the world at large as he is himself to his own circle. He feels a need to assert himself, to show his neighbours that there are other reasons, not merely fortuitous ones, which have placed him just where he is. Any of Mr. Burger's neighbours was as likely to take the same views and say the same things that he did; but at the moment they fell from his lips, in a voice which suggested the springing of a trap, he stamped them heavily as personal property. His favourite domestic amusement, from which twenty years of usage had not taken off the gloss, was to bring out wicked little things which shocked his wife and made her exclaim, "Throgmorton!" This happened pretty often.

It is possible, however, that she was not so much shocked as she appeared. If she had not been quite so buxom, or taller, she would have been very handsome, and as it was, her good looks were unquestionable—that kind of good looks which depends on an unharassed life.

She had the good sense to let the grey seam her thick black hair, without resorting to the various "refreshers" in vogue; and this hair, in contrast with the still youthful-looking, serene face, the sultry brown eyes, and full sensuous mouth, gave her a very distinctive appearance, especially of an evening, when the values were enhanced by well-shaped arms and shoulders. She had, moreover, that extremely rare gift in women—a beautifully modulated speaking voice. As with so many other Englishwomen, what an impartial observer—especially a foreign observer—would deduce from her appearance was in such flagrant contradiction with her expressed views of conduct and her abject subjection to the narrowest social code, that some might have rashly put her down as a hypocrite, and wondered when and in what company she took the mask off. But there was no mask: she lived in accordance with her professions, and apparently without effort. And after all, viewing the narrowness of the plank she walked on, some of her evolutions were astonishingly free. Doubtless she considered that if the plank was narrow, it was strong enough to bear a lot of jumping about. Indeed, just here lay the secret of her charm for most men and some women: that she was constantly promising some piquant violation of her code, while you felt all the time that she would never violate it. She took herself seriously; was, of course, a regular church-goer, and a Primrose dame; ploughed through reports of Christian Endeavour and Charity Organization Societies; and was president of the local society for the reformation of female tramps. She had a reputation for benevolence, and she was in fact perfectly willing to do people a good turn when it did not put her to any considerable inconvenience; and this, as the world goes, is about as much as one can expect.

"Is Mr. Behrens Ibed in a good mood these days?" she asked William.

The very thought of Ibed Brothers was enough to freeze whatever spirits and good-humour William had shown up to this, and to spoil his dinner. He was on the point of answering tartly that he knew nothing about Ibed and hardly ever saw him; but he thought better of it. After all, there was nothing to be gained by making himself cheap before his uncle and aunt.

"I had a long talk with him this morning," he said carelessly. "The old boy is much as usual."

"Oh fie, William, you mustn't call Mr. Ibed old!" Aunt Laura smiled, shewing her even teeth. "He is a great favourite of mine. I like him *so* much. He was with us at Monte Carlo last winter, and we saw a great deal of him."

"*You* did, you mean," put in Mr. Burger. "I'm the kind of man who don't get on with your big business swells. To tell you the truth, my boy, I find them limited—what I call limited, eh?"

"Ibed's is Limited," said William solemnly, but nobody laughed.

"Limited liability, I mean," he explained laboriously. "You know when they bust up they have to—oh, all right."

For neither of them was listening to him. Mr. Burger was frowning prodigiously at his plate, thinking perhaps of injuries he had supported from some of those "dam business fellows," and Aunt Laura was drawing pensively with her thumb-nail on the cloth.

"Yes, I like him," she pursued in her sweet voice, which made it a delight to listen to her, no matter what trash she was talking. "He's so full of fun and good-humour. He jokes about everything; you would think he hadn't a care in the world. And I'm sure, William"—she smiled again—"he doesn't seem old—well, not too old," she corrected on a low note, which was like an admirable performance ended.

But William turned on her a look of gloomy disapproval which would have checked a flow of spirits in the least sensitive. He thought her silly. For him she was only Aunt Laura, ranged with his mother and King Edward the Seventh among the souvenirs of his boyhood, the things he had always known. The only time it had occurred to him that there might be anything exceptional about her was one day, in his first years at school, when she had come to see him, and Carr, the great half-back, had pronounced favourably on her looks and asked who she was. But the effect of this was transitory, and he had long since got back to considering his aunt dispassionately, with a lean to depreciation. Besides, he didn't believe in unbending much with relations; it might encourage them to take liberties.

"Well," he said, with a short dry laugh, "I call him old because he is really. He's around forty."

"Ha, ha, ha!" Uncle Herbert was immensely amused. "Wait till you get to my age, my boy, and you won't think forty old. I'm the kind of man who thinks that for a healthy man forty is the brink of life. I say, the brink of life. It's my opinion that a man is only as old as he feels, and I'm jiggered if I feel sixty, eh?"

William grunted in a way which might mean assent, and also might not.

"William seems much older than you, Herbert," said Aunt Laura softly.

Pardonably, she found her guest dull. She usually received a good deal of sentimental attention from young men, and she had not seen this young man for so long that he was almost a stranger to her—quite enough of a stranger, certainly, for her to criticize the man apart from the nephew. The evening in the drawing-room seemed to her long, and she wished somebody would come in. She sat with her feet on the fender, talking in detached sentences to the young man, trying to interest him, to find out his interests; Uncle Herbert dozed; and William made no attempt to add to the entertainment.

"I think I shall go to bed," she said, at half-past ten. She never got angry when she was living uncomfortable moments, but to prolong them beyond the strictly necessary tick of the clock seemed to her as idiotic as to take in the shape of punishment and pain what could, by a little dexterous manipulation, be turned into a pleasure. "I want you to light my candle for me, William," she resumed. "Come on upstairs."

On the first floor she turned into a little sitting-room where a rose-coloured lamp shed a dim light, and settled herself in one of the deep chairs.

"Bring up that chair near me," she directed William. "I want to talk to you seriously."

She smiled disarmingly to take the edge off the word, but William sat down solemn, with his brow furrowed. He was rather alarmed: what was he going to be bothered about now?

"You know Sabina Moll is coming?"

So that was all! "Yes; you said so in your letter."

"To-morrow afternoon. Now, listen to me, William. I want you to be very, very nice to her."

"Oh, I'll be all right." He made an effort. "What does she do specially?"

"Well"—Aunt Laura hesitated, vaguely smiling. "She is very fond of walking."

"Walking!" William did not warm up. "Doesn't she play any games or anything?"

"I think she played a little tennis when she was here last summer, and they say she is quite good at croquet."

There was a pause. Aunt Laura moved a little forward and put her soft hand, shining with rings, on William's huge knuckles.

"What a great big fellow you are for a nephew!"

Here, there was room for a compliment, but William did not place it. With her usual good-nature Aunt Laura overlooked the omission, and developed her little scheme for his benefit.

"Listen, William. You are quite old enough to be married. Wouldn't it be nice if you got to care for Sabina?"

William twisted around in his chair and snatched his hand away. "But I can't marry her!" he blurted out.

Aunt Laura drew back, alarmed. "You haven't made a fool of yourself in London?"

William had already seen his mistake. "Oh Lord, no," he said easily.

She drew a breath of relief. "My dear William, you don't know her yet. She is really very nice."

"I suppose so." William was pondering with his eyes fixed on the wall. "Is Sabina Moll anything like her father?"

"Like her father?" Aunt Laura laughed musically. "You absurd boy! Poor Sabina! No, I don't think she is very like her father."

"Well, that scores in her favour," said William. "I don't want to say anything against any friend of yours, Aunt Laura, but old Mr. Moll——"

"Ssh!" Aunt Laura again put her hand out, this time on his sleeve. "You mustn't, you wicked wretch. He's awfully rich. Simply rolling. Of course most of his fortune will go to his sons; but do you know that Sabina is going to have at least four thousand a year?"

Whatever other faults might be laid to William's charge, nobody could impute to him a disregard for his own interests. Brought up among the shifts of narrow means, and under conditions which often threw him among the luxuries of the well-to-do, he had come to look on poverty as the sole evil under the sun, and almost as a crime. Frankly and cordially, he despised people who had no money. He would have despised himself if he had ever thought that he was always going to be poor. He had but the vaguest notions how his condition was to be remedied, but he felt certain it would be—mainly, I suppose, because he considered it ought to be. The injustice of his lot was too flagrant not to obtain redress. He looked at his aunt with more respect and friendliness than he had shown since he had entered the house. There was one thing to be said for Aunt Laura: she knew how to keep in with rich people.

"Your mother would be so much pleased if anything came of it," she continued. "It would make such a difference. There would be no more clerking at Ibed's, for instance."

She had at last uttered the telling note with that mellifluous tongue of hers. After his ignominious departure from the office that morning, William's strongest desire was never to see Ibed's again. Coming down in the train, thinking over his battered dignity, he had almost determined to "chuck it." Exaggerating, as most of us do, the importance of the position he occupied in the lives of other people, he could only picture the clerks constantly thinking about him, impatiently awaiting his return for new enterprises of wit, devising in their leisure hours ridiculous situations for him and his aunt. For one who had so long taken his stand as the young superior god of the office, to drop to the mere butt was too galling: how could he ever stand it? What worse fall than that of the man who finds the chair in which he sits self-satisfied, confident of admiration, suddenly plucked from under him? No; Ibed's would never see him again if he could help it. Where would he find another post? How was he to live meanwhile? And there came singing into his ears, in his aunt's beautiful voice, the name of Sabina Moll and her four thousand a year.

He sat silent so long that Aunt Laura imagined him weighing foolish, unimportant questions of Sabina's looks and capacity for out-door exercise. In reality, he was entangled in much more abstruse perplexities, weaving plots, estimating chances so dark that, easy as she was, if she had known them she must have cried out in horror. After a little, he glanced up at her with a smile.

"I believe Sabina and I will hit it off, Aunt Laura."

Recognizing all the concessions underlying these words, she diplomatically left the matter there, and rose. "I ought to be in bed. I shall lose all my beauty if you keep me up like this. Be off at once, you abominable youth!" Then, over her shoulder as he was going: "I expect you're glad there's no more Ibed's for some time?"

"Oh, I don't know," William drawled. "Good night, Aunt Laura."

As she put out the rose-coloured lamp she had two thoughts. The first was one which has occurred to all great founders, organizers and projectors in all ages of the world, impatient of the inadequate tools they have to work with. And the second was, that there were at least four men whom she liked much better than William, into whose hands she would have steered Sabina Moll and her fortune with much more pleasure. But then they were not her nephews.

Chapter III

"LET OTHER PEOPLE TALK as they like," said Mr. Burger, throwing aside the newspaper, "I always maintain that a good brisk walk after breakfast is an excellent thing—I say, a most excellent thing. What do you think of a stroll down to the town?"

He looked at William. Aunt Laura seldom appeared in the mornings. A house which ran so easily and comfortably must have been carefully supervised, but it was characteristic of that amiable woman that the supervision was not noticeable. And it was characteristic of the two men—the uncle clad in light grey, William in a blue serge coat, white flannel trousers, and patent-leather pumps, both bare-headed, both smoking pipes—that they should grumble at her as they sauntered along.

"What I say your aunt ought to do is to get out in the morning and go for a long walk. I'm always telling her that. She's getting so fat. She never walks anywhere. Stays in bed half the morning, and motors or drives when she goes out. Now, what I say is, that sort of thing ain't wholesome—I say, not wholesome. How do you think she's looking?" he asked, falling into that melancholy error of the middle-aged; for healthy youth seldom observes people from the point of view of their health or welfare, and selfish youth never.

"She seems all right," replied William carelessly.

"She never puts one foot before the other," insisted the uncle.

"Jolly slack life," says William.

Thus pleasantly conversing, they entered the town. As they passed through the streets, Mr. Burger nodded amicably right and left, and meanwhile explained to William some of the town's idiosyncrasies.

"The Fords live there—nice people, not very well off, branch of the Fords of Starke Abbey. I dare say they'll ask us in some evening soon. This red-brick house is old Parry's, the banker. He lives there with his three daughters, old maids as ugly as the devil, always cutting up flannel. But rich, my boy—ten per centers."

"That's a very fine house over there," said William, pointing.

"H'm," mumbled Uncle Herbert dubiously. "Yes, I suppose it's fine enough. Ought to be, if money can do it. We don't go there. It belongs to Corder—you've heard of Corder who has the boot and shoe stores at Portsmouth, Southampton, all over the place? I meet him sometimes at the station and round about, but your aunt draws the line at the family."

"Well, after all," decided William, "boots and shoes, you know—retail too—Aunt Laura can't be expected to swallow that."

He soon learned that society at Palebrook was quite as exclusive as he could wish. Rigid lines divided people between whom there was really no difference, except perhaps a better acquaintance with the rules governing certain castes. The cream was a composition of the families of a few retired Service men, of people living on their incomes, like the Burgers, of the coastguard lieutenant, the parson, the banker, and their belongings. To these were to be added a few elderly men, living in lodgings or small houses on the outskirts of the town, who were always hanging about, had always endless vacant hours on their hands, and were classified by the tradespeople as "retired gentlemen." The Corders and other families in businesses that were inelegant, although just as intelligent and well-mannered as the others, were barred out, and, what is more, did not seem to resent the insufferable insolence and condescension with which they were treated, but rather took it submissively, hoping in patience for some far-off lucky day when they would be accepted by the *élite*. It was even currently reported that the young Corders were ashamed of their father's business which kept them in opulence.

You could hardly find a better proof of the truth of Pascal's maxim, that the value one attaches to the opinion of a town depends upon the length of time one stays in it; for to the mere passer, the casual observer, to be received in Palebrook society seemed about the most undesirable thing in the world. Meanwhile, the sons of the *élite*, coming down from the Universities, from Sandhurst, and the public schools, in vacation time, did all they could to intensify the class consciousness by excluding the sons of all those below the salt from whatever sports or entertainments were forward. The public tennis courts, for instance, of the two parties lay together, divided by a rather low wall, and there they segregated themselves from each other in a remarkable manner. Nothing was more comic than to watch them on a summer afternoon, when a ball, occasionally dropping into a wrong court, was tossed back, and received with a lofty "Oh thanks!" on the one side, and a "Thank *you!*" respectfully uttered with an undertone of grievance on the other.

Below these jarring factions were the small shopkeepers—Dissenters, for the most part, and fierce Radicals. Then, over the whole town loomed the shadow of the Marquess of Wednesbury, whose seat was about a mile away. Although this nobleman and his family never showed the slightest interest in the place, although they made a point of not knowing a soul in it except the lawyer who had to do with the estate, although few in the town could say for certain when his lordship was at Palebrook Court, his name for all that had an enormous effect upon the community—on that part of it, at all events, with which we are mainly concerned. It was said he used to boast that if he wanted to raise money for any affair, he had only to let it be known in Palebrook that the scheme had his patronage and the subscriptions poured in. "Palebrook may yell against the House of Lords at election times," he said again, "but those are only the scum of the people and Dissenters. You take my word for it, Palebrook is one of the strongholds of old English snobbery. Very proper thinking people down there. When I represented the division I had a majority in the town every time, simply because the well-to-do people put the lid on the shopkeepers by saying they'd get all their stuff from the Stores in London if the place voted wrong." Possibly his attitude towards the town was the outcome of a deep policy. There was no valid reason for asking one Palebrook family to his house more than another, and if he asked one, he would be obliged (unless he wished to rouse a turmoil of jealousy) to ask the lot. Besides, by secluding himself as he did at present, he made something of the same impression on Palebrook as Queen Victoria by the same means is said to have made on the nation at large.

At the turn of the street, Mr. Burger nudged his nephew. "Here! we'll speak to this person, William. He's a regular character." And in a moment William was introduced to the Reverend Arthur Smalt, who gave him a chill hand, and looked at him oddly, with little green cruel eyes, set in a head made up of close-growing white hair, a wrinkled, obstinate-looking forehead, a short red nose, a weak, querulous mouth, and a stubborn chin. Clean-shaven, all these traits were unrelieved;

and the expression of his face was a blend of obstinacy, ill-temper, dyspepsia and disappointment.

"Why can't people keep themselves clean?" he asked arrogantly, looking hard at William, who began to wonder whether he should not resent this remark as a personal insult.

"Lord bless me, I don't know!" Mr. Burger put in hastily. "I try to myself."

"I've just been visiting dirty brats and their ignobly unclean mothers. Parishioners," says the parson with a bitter smile. "Are you afraid of croup? Do you shrink from whooping-cough? They are both stalking in this abominable borough."

"I don't think I'm quite old enough for those things, vicar," Mr. Burger said with a grin. "In a few years I'll take more precautions. But we have three doctors here. Can't they—"

"Oh, doctors!" The vicar tossed his head in contempt. "I have no faith in doctors."

Miss Parry was passing and held up a warning finger. "Now, Mr. Smalt, no theology!" The vicar left the two men and joined her.

"That's what I call an odd fish," said Mr. Burger with a chuckle when the vicar had passed on. "He's the terror of the bishops. He's been in three dioceses. He's been in the Church, and out of it, and now he's back again. He's always disputing and writing to the *Times*, and whenever he changes his opinion he writes a book about it. We're Broad Church here at present, but he began High. He lives alone up there in that mouldy old vicarage with a brace of dogs that he scourges unmercifully, and his two terrors are that somebody will borrow money from him, or that some acquaintance of his will turn up that he'll be obliged to give a bed to. Best joke was that he ran away to London last year because he heard some friend of his, who was rather badly off, was coming to Palebrook. The friend came, and stayed at the inn all the time. Very decent fellow, too. I went fishing with him one day."

"But why do you keep such a blighter?" William asked.

"Keep him? We don't keep him. He's some kind of connexion of the Wednesburys, and the Marquess gave him the living. But they're afraid of their lives of him. They won't let him within a mile of the house. The only time he was there, he kept correcting the servants, and said their cooking was poisonous. Shouldn't be surprised if he was right about that." Uncle Herbert pulled out his watch. "Come, let's go back. I'm a great man for lunch—lunch is what I call an important meal."

On their way, they passed by a charming Queen Anne house which stood at some distance from the road, amid well-kept lawns and gardens. Just as they went by the gate, there came forth a dark, lean man of a pale visage, who hung his clothes on somewhat slovenly.

"Hullo, Stephen!" sang out Mr. Burger; "mind you come in to-night! We expect Sabina Moll this afternoon—your friend of last year."

The other stopped, and William disliked him at once; for although he had never seen Sabina Moll, his thoughts were upon her, and it galled him that any woman in whom he deigned to interest himself should be interested in others. Besides, there was something particularly antipathetic to him in this man with the clean-shaven, professional face, dark, clear-cut, and hard, whose unruffled, concentrated manner and bleak smile as he glanced at the youth implied some vague assumption of superiority and advantage. Instinctively, William felt that the brief, keen look from the stranger's black eyes was an attempt to sum him up, and that the judgment was not on the whole a favourable one. He had been so used from childhood to being petted, to have people make way for him and consult his moods, that any lack of the usual deference made him feel small, and whenever he was made to feel small he became morose.

"Who is that bounder?" he asked his uncle as they walked on.

"Bounder! My dear boy, how do you expect to succeed in life? Why, that's Stephen Ruggles, our great man. Hand and glove with the Wednesburys, and all that. Quite a personage, I assure you. They've been lawyers in Palebrook for ages. That fine house he came out of—that's his house. They say his ancestor built it in the time of Queen Anne, whenever that was. You're later from school than I am."

William strode ahead, sucking at his pipe, which was out. "Is he married?" he asked, after a bit.

"No, he is not. He'll be a good catch for somebody."

"It's about time she caught him if she's going to," said William, and added a disagreeable laugh. "He's old enough."

"Yes," said Uncle Herbert, ruminating. "I suppose he must be somewhere between thirty and forty."

Chapter IV

WILLIAM ATE A HEAVY lunch, and then drowsed away the afternoon under the trees on the lawn, a jar of tobacco on the grass by his side, and a heap of illustrated papers and magazines, with a new novel on top to keep them from fluttering. About five o'clock a motorcar, driven by Mr. Burger, came through the gate, and on the back seat of this were a lady, and a nurse in uniform.

"Whew!" William whistled and his eyes darkened. "She's an invalid. If that's not about the limit! I won't marry a medicine bottle—simply won't, that's all about it. Aunt Laura might have warned me, I think. I'm going on strike."

But the car stopped, and the lady jumped out without any signs of feebleness. William from his distance watched Aunt Laura kiss her on the threshold, and then draw her into the house.

"She's small," William criticized. "She doesn't come up to Aunt Laura's shoulder, and she's not a tall woman. I rather like short girls; they're a change." He rose and stretched himself. "I suppose I had better show up. They'll all be wondering where I am and waiting for me to appear. I wonder why they didn't send the motor for me yesterday instead of that feeble cab thing?"

Laughter sounded from the drawing-room, and voices in brisk conversation. William, who had half imagined that they would be sitting in awkward impatience, anxiously expecting his arrival, felt rather disappointed. "They seem to be enjoying themselves," he thought resentfully. Then he coughed loud to attract attention and went in. Two other ladies from the neighbourhood were there, but Uncle Herbert was the only man.

"Ah, here's William," said Aunt Laura, hardly turning her head, and she went on with her conversation.

William stood about, and to show himself at ease attempted to start a talk with his uncle; but the uncle was listening amused to what the ladies were saying and gave him hardly any attention. It was very trying.

Sabina sat lost in a big chair with her feet scarcely touching the floor, and from the depths of the chair she talked calmly in a flat, rather hesitating voice. She wore a big white hat, and underneath it appeared a face which did not strike William as particularly pretty. She seemed older than he had thought she would be, and, remembering the nurse, he wondered if it were the effect of disease. But after a few minutes he was set right on that point.

"I don't mind so much having measles," Sabina was saying. "It's not at all a painful malady, do you think? At least not the way I had it. But I always fancy everybody is inclined to laugh. They think it's such a childish thing to have measles when one is grown up."

She smiled, and it was a rather mirthless smile. From the way one corner of the mouth went up it might even be called bitter; yet it was not unpleasant to see, because it managed to convey that whatever dissatisfaction the smile indicated was applied to herself more than to others. Her face was moulded on the same small plan as her body, and although it had not a single good feature, it yet managed to be what is called "pleasing." But this impression was due more to her still, unassertive manner than to any distinct quality revealed; for there was no sensibility in her face and little good-nature, perhaps because she had never found occasions in her life which called for the steady exercise of these virtues. Still, she had as a rule those very amiable and conciliating looks and manners which many young women now cultivate as a lesson to the women of a former generation whose method has been the offhand and the downright, and even the overpowering highhand, in social intercourse. The impression you took from her person and manner was of a woman who had moved along from the cradle protected by a bodyguard of guineas, and consequently had never come in touch with any real thing in life, of which she was, for all practical purposes, as ignorant as when she was a baby. She looked anything between twenty and twenty-five; at night she looked scarcely the first, in the daytime fully the last, and in trying lights, or at moments when her nerves and digestion were wrong, considerably older.

William, feeling extremely snubbed, sat unnoticed till the two callers rose to go away. He strolled through the window out on the lawn chafing, and when he came back found Sabina by herself looking at a magazine.

She raised her eyes quickly and then fixed them on her book again. "Do you know this part of Hampshire?" she asked after a little, without looking up.

"Oh yes, fairly well. That is, I've been down here a couple of times before. I don't care about Hampshire. I've biked through Yorkshire," he added.

This did not seem to interest Sabina, who made some inarticulate sound and turned over a page of her magazine.

"I am thinking of flying," said William after a minute. His voice was full of importance. As a matter of fact it had only just that moment occurred to him, but he thought it quite an idea.

Sabina raised her eyebrows. She looked sincerely puzzled. "Flying? Wherever to?" Somehow her tone implied that she expected to be entertained by seeing him take flight then and there.

William waved an arm vaguely to convey the vast reaches of space. "In an aerodrome, I suppose. I should need a few lessons first."

"Oh *that!*" said Sabina, losing interest. "You seem rather solid, don't you? Or does that not matter?" And once more she became absorbed in her magazine. William was wondering whether he wouldn't let her go to blazes, when, after a long enough pause, she spoke again.

"I've just had the measles," she said, "and your aunt thought this air would suit me."

He looked at her solemnly, thinking there was some chance she might still have it about her clothes. "Beastly selfishness!" he reflected. "If I catch measles it will spoil my holiday." Then a reassuring thought followed, and he spoke.

"I had measles when I was at school. It got me off a term. I don't believe you can get it twice."

"No?" queried Sabina; and there was silence again.

"It takes people differently," William put in after another minute.

"What does?"

"Measles."

"Oh!"

William shifted his legs and said he supposed she liked the country.

"Oh, anything is a change from Manchester. I hate Manchester!" She got up and stood for a little with a curious swaying motion of her little body and arms, such as a schoolgirl often has when she recites her lesson. In Sabina it was not graceful. She moved some things on a table near her, kicked the toe of one shoe with the heel of the other, and then went out of the room rather awkwardly and left William fuming. Her repellent manner, which a person with any powers of observation would have at once put down to intense shyness, seemed to him the insolence of the wealthy woman. "Of course, she knows I'm in Ibed's and she thinks I'm not good enough to talk to. She puts me in with her old father's beastly little clerks. I never met such a disagreeable woman. Nobody would stand her if she wasn't rich. But I'll show her a thing or two."

Young as he was, and although he knew more or less intimately several girls round about his own age, yet he was far from being in unison with some of our modern lights where women were concerned. The woman he always took his bearings by was the woman of thirty-five or forty years ago: that for him was a permanent type. Present-day aspects of the feminine spirit he either ignored, or regarded as sickening divergences from the proper type. That woman's development had been hampered was an abstract proposition in which he took no interest; if he had thought about it at all, he would have agreed that she was long ago fully developed on all the points where development could profitably take place. That any woman was in any way that mattered the equal of man was to him unthinkable, and his opinion of women who assumed masculine airs was the meanest, while the men who approved such travesties were either silly juveniles or senile.

Accordingly, at dinner that evening he attempted to show Sabina many things, and first of all that he was a rather important person. There is no stronger conviction among the professional classes in the British Isles than that they have a right to treat with some contempt the possessors of fortunes made in trade; and this feeling, when they are themselves reduced to Government pensions and narrow incomes, aids them enormously in maintaining their self-esteem when they are brought in contact with new-got wealth. William set out to show Sabina Moll, indirectly of course, that people like the Moll family might consider themselves honoured and lucky beyond their wildest hopes by an alliance with the son of a deceased Lieutenant-Colonel.

"There's a friend of mine in town," he said, addressing his uncle with studied carelessness—"Clement Stagg, son of Stagg, the captain of H.M.S. *Irrecoverable*, who nearly got engaged to Flavour's daughter last year—I mean, the Flavour of Flavour and Blades, the Oxford Street tradesmen. They're millionaires, but Clem's mater and sisters simply wouldn't hear of the match."

At dinner-time, beyond a perfunctory performance of his duties as host, reduced to their simplest forms when the party was an intimate one, Uncle Herbert seldom paid much attention to what was going forward. Now he simply answered: "Indeed? God bless my soul!" as one who dreams, staring meanwhile anxiously at a dish presented to him. But Aunt Laura looked at William with troubled eyes, and thought that all her plans must crumble if the foolish boy could not be stopped. She considered her nephew with the feelings of a playwright who watches a drunken actor disorganize his play. What in the world would he knock over next?

He was now offering himself as the hardened man of the world, familiar with the devious ways of London life; he talked of theatres, and music-halls, and related anecdotes of "celebrities" which he had heard from one of the clerks who had had a maiden aunt on the stage, or recollected from the gossiping columns of the newspapers.

"I have seldom been at the theatre," said Sabina in a prim voice which seemed meant to convey that she was tired of the subject. "I suppose there are theatres in Manchester, but I have not been in them."

"Oh, my dear!" protested Aunt Laura to keep William quiet. "How very strange of you! There is a Manchester school of acting. Alicia Ford was telling me all about it the other day. They are the same as the Irish—or rather I don't think they're *quite* the same; but they make you see things that weren't there before, and all that. Awfully interesting."

"Of course there are Manchester actors," William declared emphatically. He mentioned a well-known comic singer. "He was born in Manchester. His brother told me."

"I much prefer concerts, don't you?" Sabina asked Aunt Laura. And she went on to explain that she liked attending travellers' lectures. "There was an awfully interesting man who gave a lecture on Japan one afternoon last February. Effie Patten, my Newnham College friend, was greatly captivated. She wanted us to go off there together, but father, as usual, wouldn't allow it."

"What a pity! It would have been so nice for you," said Aunt Laura soothingly. But William broke in:

"Did you mean to go alone?"

Sabina opened her eyes a little. "Yes; just my friend and I."

He was put to it to stifle a guffaw. His dislike of her was blending into contempt and pity. And he began to talk of his own travels, which had, however, been limited to England, the northern coast of France, and Lausanne. He held forth grandly on hotels, as he was used to do with the clerks at Ibed's; but his aunt, who guessed on what terms his mother had stayed at such places, looked hot and ashamed, and even Mr. Burger, when he was at leisure to listen, began to fidget.

"I know nothing about English hotels," said Sabina.

She spoke as if she were denying a knowledge of saloon-bars, and William, taking this as another example of her narrowness, enjoyed a moment of triumph. But the obvious embarrassment of the table gained upon him. For his aunt's uneasiness he cared nothing; she was only a woman, and, so far as he could see, a silly one. William liked the company of young women—in fact, he was rather a philanderer—but this sentiment kept house with a good, sound, Tory, Old Testament contempt for women as acting and thinking creatures, and he was possessed by the misguided notion that a man can argue a woman in or out of anything. But his uncle too appeared uneasy, and that was more serious. It was enough to check the flow of William's talk, which had been running so fluently. His spirits fell; a horrible suspicion dawned on him that he was not being admired and envied so much as he thought; and under the shock he saw a new meaning in Sabina's last remark. This he was now inclined to twist into the boast of a purse-proud woman, who is not subject to the accidents of common travellers, but has a private house to receive her wherever she stops. And for one moment he had an intolerable vision of Sabina, whom he so much wished to regard with contemptuous familiarity, moving among the haunts of the enormously wealthy, on social heights he could never hope to attain.

The vision was too poignant to last, and he told himself angrily it was nonsense; but it had shaken him for all that, and he carried the effects of it into the drawing-room, even as one carries dim effects of a nightmare out into a sunshine morning amid the labours of the day. Various people had come in: old Parry with his daughters, active, elderly, solemn women without physical attractions; the coastguard lieutenant, a disputatious, shouldering sort of man, who had a conviction that he was socially and in most other ways superior to the people he came in contact with at Palebrook, accompanied by his wife, a pretty Irishwoman, whose existence was passed in suckling babies and backing up her husband's assertions. Stephen Ruggles and five or six others made up the residue.

A stout girl played the "Carnival of Venice" on the piano with what was called "brilliant execution." Her sister combined with her then in a *duo* for piano and violin. Sabina was asked to play or sing. She swung over to the piano shyly and ungracefully, and Ruggles managed to throw two more cushions on the piano-stool without being observed, which saved her the embarrassment of asking for them. In her gratitude she gave him a look which established an understanding between them at once. Seated thus at the piano under the shaded lights, she looked attractive, with her flushed face, her hair made the most of, and red flowers in her dark hair. Her hands and arms too, on which she wore a good deal of jewellery, although they were heavily shaped, revealing no sign of fine stock in the Moll pedigree, were white and firm. Under her very thick eyebrows, which grew into a perverse tuft near the nose and indicated a considerable amount of animal passion and temper in the little body, her soft brown eyes glanced up timidly at Ruggles, who stood by her, watching the music over her shoulder. And as princesses of royal blood are called handsome on easier terms than other people—there being always the reservation understood: "handsome for a Royalty"—so Sabina Moll in a shrine of pounds sterling seemed wonderfully pretty, though had you met her in an omnibus or behind the counter of a shop she might have struck you as insignificant. She played, and then she sang, and the way she did both revealed the fact that her father had spent some money to have her taught, and nothing more. She was not even on a level with the usual drawing-room and village-concert amateur. It was better not to hear such playing and singing.

William moved about with his eyes on her, almost glowering at her. It was not that he had the least symptom of any feeling which could be capitulated under the term amorous for Sabina Moll; there were girls here far prettier than she was and with whom he felt he could get along much better; but he had been so used hitherto to being cajoled and sought after by young women that he could not sit easy under her indifference. His aunt, to anchor him, set him to playing Bridge. He had no excuse to refuse; but ere long he trumped his own trick when he was playing both hands, and shortly after revoked, which caused his partner, Miss Parry, a punctilious player, to call him to order in severe terms. Thereupon good-natured Aunt Laura, who was for putting everybody at ease, came up offering to play his hand, and desired him to go and talk to Sabina.

William lounged up to her and began a conversation on songs. He mentioned the ones he liked and the singers he had heard sing them.

The names were unfamiliar to Sabina, and William showed his surprise a little too emphatically.

"I'm afraid I've not had your advantages," Sabina dropped icily, with the little dry laugh which usually followed when she said something disagreeable.

William, however, was better armoured against such shafts than she guessed, and he accepted the remark literally. It was only too plain that she hadn't had his advantages! But he judged it well to change the conversation. He thought her stupid; but if she wanted serious and stodgy topics he was her man.

"Are you interested in politics?" he asked portentously.

"Very much," replied Sabina; but she proceeded to talk of contemporary questions in a way which was less than vague. Still, William was not much beforehand, and they might have got on very well with this subject, being both too ignorant of its details to fight over it, when Sabina faced him suddenly.

"No doubt you support the suffrage for women?"

William was flabbergasted. If she had asked him whether he was in favour of letting loose the lunatics in Bedlam he would not have been so much astounded. Although this question and the situation in Ireland were the two matters which just at that moment overshadowed all others in British politics, his experience had never brought him in contact with any women who regarded it seriously, and it had been presented to him from the music-hall and musical-comedy stage, where the Suffragette was looked on as a catch for a laugh as certain as the henpecked husband, the foreigner, the long-haired or bald-headed man, and the policeman. He knew that such people as Suffragettes must exist in reality elsewhere than on the stage or parading the streets, but it had never occurred to him to picture them in civilized conditions, any more than the dancing restaurant-keepers, gay dressmakers, or other phantoms of the theatre.

He looked hard at her, suspiciously, to see if she was not trying to make a fool of him; but when he was satisfied that she was really serious he gave a contemptuous laugh.

"Do you mean the Votes for Women lot? I should jolly well think I don't support them. Why, everybody knows that they're absolutely mad. You've only got to look at them." And his mind presented a lank creature with short pale hair, dressed in broad checks, and with a pair of spectacles spanning a red nose. "You don't really believe in them yourself, do you?"

Sabina looked deeply hurt. "Of course I do," she answered crossly. She began to flounder through some arguments, trying to reconstruct the logical chain of proofs which she had so often heard her Newnham College friend, Effie Patten, adduce, but it was only too evident that she was not very well up in the polemics of the subject.

Ruggles drew near and supported her. He had overheard the dispute, and he professed to be a convinced advocate for women's enfranchisement. He pointed out the number of women who paid taxes, who managed households, who were the real breadwinners, and he quoted figures. He advanced some other stock arguments. He saw that neither of his hearers knew anything about the matter, and as he wished to please Sabina, who, he guessed, had thrown herself in with the party simply because some friend or friends of hers had done so, what he said became a sort of *argumentum ad invidiam*.

He looked better in evening dress than he had in the morning. He was straight and well-knit; his thick smooth black hair threw into relief the face, thin and pallid, which was not, however, the pallor of ill-health. What was perhaps the strangest thing about him was that when he smiled, which he did often, the smile was limited to the beautifully shaped mouth, while the eyes remained serious. His face, taken altogether, had that look of artificiality which is often seen on the faces of actors, and politicians, and law-counsel, men who counterfeit emotions, who live in the sight of the public and depend on the public applause.

William thought that Ruggles had come up purposely to insult him in the presence of Sabina. He did not believe there was a man in England who sincerely backed the female suffrage. And as he thus regarded the whole dispute as personal, he tried to take a fall out of Ruggles, hauling down bits of argument, scraps of information from dusty shelves of memory where they had somehow stuck. He recalled a news-placard he had seen of one of the evening papers.

"Look what Lloyd George said in the House!"

Ruggles smiled with irritating blandness. "Yes; what *did* Lloyd George say?"

William was floored. He had no more idea than the man in the moon—or Sabina. But she was looking up at Ruggles with undisguised admiration, and William went in for him again, talking very loud.

"I don't care; I tell you I've seen them. Possibly you haven't. I've seen them at Westminster, trying to pull down the House of Commons and being hauled off by the bobbies." His innate contempt for women added bitterness to his tongue. "You don't propose to hand over the government of the country to that kind of a lot, do you? No sensible man does, at least. What good would they be in time of war?"

"I should have thought," said Ruggles suavely, "that that's just what they have shown themselves fit for, from what you've been telling us."

Old Parry, the banker, coming up at the moment, burst into a loud laugh, and Sabina turned away. The banker had an anecdote to relate, and he was a circumstantial teller of a story. It was impossible to continue the dispute, and William retired in sullen disgust. "I had the best of it," he thought; "but they all lick that fellow's boots here. He's about clever enough to impress Palebrook. There isn't a man to be found in London, or anywhere else in England, I don't believe, who supports those fools of Suffragettes. It isn't manly, that's all about it."

With such thoughts he solaced himself during the rest of an evening which for the others seemed to go pleasantly, and for him in spasms of chagrin and wounded vanity and what he called a sensation of being hopelessly bored. Meanwhile Aunt Laura, who had missed nothing of all this, sighed as she thought that youth is often the greatest disadvantage of the young.

Chapter V

BUT BIOGRAPHERS AND HISTORIANS assure us that it is at moments when defeat seems certain that the genius of your hero and statesman shines out brightest. Aunt Laura, lying in bed, gave her thoughts to the situation as it actually was, and came down next morning determined to set a new face on it. She put herself in the way of William about half-past eleven, just as the young man was strolling down to Palebrook.

"Are you going out, William?"

"Yes. I thought I might run across the Ford girls. Uncle says—"

"Don't go for a minute. Come and sit out of doors with me while Sabina is getting ready. We are lunching with the Bartlets about five miles from here."

She dropped into a deep chair and stared at the sky, and in her charming mauve and lace frock and big straw hat she looked fresh and smiling as if she had not a care in the world.

"What a divine morning!" She breathed it in. "And how are you getting on with Sabina?"

William had woken with half a headache, convinced that he would never get on with Sabina, and that he did not care. "I don't think we have much in common," he said. "She seems rather narrow. I've determined to leave her to herself as much as possible."

His aunt looked at him reproachfully. "How can you be so foolish! Really, William, I thought you were a man, and you act like a very child."

William, as a rule, used his youth as a bludgeon; but although he rejoiced in his youth in the fullest sense, he did not care about being called a child. Aunt Laura saw a sullen look creeping over his face.

"You must know you do yourself," she added softly. "I believe you are doing it on purpose."

"Doing what?" asked William, astonished.

"Why, making Sabina cross."

William simply jumped at this unjust charge ladled out so coolly. "Making her cross? It's the other way about, I think."

"Rubbish!" She glanced him over serenely. "How could a little thing like that make a huge fellow like you cross?"

"I think that's rather steep," grumbled William. "It has nothing to do with size. I can't strike it up with her, that's all. We're not made for each other. Besides, there's Ruggles, I suppose you've noticed? He's the whole thing, it seems to me."

"No, he's not—at least, not yet. But I admit there's some danger. I don't believe Stephen is a bit in love with her, or Sabina with him; but she may be in love with him any day, and he may be in love with four thousand a year——" Aunt Laura fell a-musing.

"What a pig!" cried William. "I thought he was rich."

"Oh, rich!" She gazed at the whispering leaves. "I suppose none of us object to increase our incomes. You'll have to change your tactics, my young prince."

"I don't see what more I can do," he put in.

"You'll have to change your tactics. The world doesn't come ready-made even to the most important of us. I had a long talk with Sabina last night in her bedroom, and I've thought the matter out. I'm going to tell you what you ought to do. I find that Sabina has become very serious: there's a friend of hers, some girl in Manchester, whom she tries to live up to. All she cares about at present are heavy things like politics and concerts and poetry——"

"Poetry?" repeated William in a dull voice.

"Poetry. So, you see, your conversation so far has been hardly of a kind to interest her. You must give up talking about race-courses and actresses and drinking-bars——"

"I never talked about drinking-bars." William flushed indignantly.

"Didn't you? Anyhow, what you must try to talk about in future are serious subjects. I expect you don't care much for such things, but you've got a good enough head, and you can manage quite easily, because she has only just begun too: she was quite ordinary last year, quite like the rest of us. Now I've picked out some books that my brother-in-law, the headmaster, left here years ago, and they've been lying about the attics ever since; but I've had them dusted and put in your room. They seem to be poetry and history and that kind of thing. You see, you can study them, and then you can tell her what you've studied. It's quite simple."

William did not think so. "Do you mean I'm to spend my holidays swotting over poetry and history?" he inquired, looking at her gloomily.

"There's Sabina! I must fly. Perhaps," she said airily, "you prefer to be a clerk at Ibed's all your life. Your mother can leave you nothing. Good-bye, William; see that they give you all you want." And she moved over the sward, a picture of grace, swinging her parasol negligently.

※

She had routed William. Her mention of Ibed's had the effect of checking any tendency to rebellion. Between the chance of four thousand a year and an ignominious return to Ibed's, who could debate? He got up and stretched himself. "I suppose I'm in for it." And he decided to go upstairs and examine the books.

There were about a dozen. Swinburne's *Poems and Ballads*, *John Inglesant*, Pater's *Imaginary Portraits*, FitzGerald's *Omar Khayyám*, Charles Kingsley's *Poems*, were among them. William opened one after the other in despair. How was he ever going to get any grip on such stuff? But fully conscious of all that depended on the business, he set himself doggedly to plough through some pages, and possessing, as Aunt Laura had said, a good enough head, he managed to subdue a certain amount of unruly matter to his intelligence.

After lunch he was at it again with commendable assiduity, leaving his uncle, with whom he had lunched, in consternation.

"But you said you'd come sailing, William?"

"Yes, but I want to read."

In that house, to put off anything for the sake of reading was unheard of. There was only one way to account for it, and Uncle Herbert looked at him anxiously.

"I think you said you have had the measles, didn't you?"

William nodded as he lit his pipe, adding that he felt all right.

"But God bless my soul, to stay in the house on a fine afternoon like this! It's quite possible you've picked up that affair from Sabina. It's very catching. Perhaps Whitmore had better have a look at you. I call him a thoroughly sound practitioner. A little too given to the bed-and-slops dodge for my taste, but safe and sound. I'll speak to your aunt about it to-night. You don't feel like walking down to him now, eh?"

Finally, he was left to his studies. About half-past four, glancing out of the window, he saw that Sabina had returned and was drifting through the garden alone.

He went out and strolled abstractedly in her direction, reading in his book—the *Imaginary Portraits*. As he drew near, he seemed to perceive her and started violently. He really did it very well.

"I was so taken up with my book," he explained.

"Is it a detective story?" Sabina asked slightingly. "I thought you had gone on the water with Mr. Burger."

"Yes, I was to have gone, but this is my day for study. I stayed in and read." A glow of no ill-founded pride came into his face as he said this, thinking of the abominable stuff he had wrestled with all the afternoon. Few men could do the same.

Sabina looked at him uncertainly. "Was your book so very interesting?"

"I don't know that people in general would find it interesting," William answered loftily. "It interested me. Or rather they did. I do not," he remarked pointedly, "confine myself to one book."

For the first time since they had met, Sabina had a slight sense of inferiority. That he had stayed in to whistle, to dance, to stand on his head—anything of that kind she would have heard from William with such equanimity as we have for the not altogether unexpected. But that he had stayed in to read, and to read out-of-the-way, serious books! She looked at him with a certain timidity which was something quite different from her habitual shyness.

"What is the name of your book?"

He showed her the title-page, with his heart in his mouth. Suppose she had read it—had mastered the stodgy pages!

"*Imaginary Portraits,*" she murmured respectfully. "Walter Pater. Is he a great author?"

William breathed again. He felt kindly to the unknown Pater: she had never heard of Pater, so Pater had saved him. "I should rather think so. One of the best."

"Pater," she mused. "What a very odd name. I have never heard Effie Patten talk of him. I should be sure to remember if I had," and her little face looked strained and anxious.

"Rather deep for women," said William mysteriously. "Rather off it, I can tell you. It even takes me all my time to follow him. So you see——"

"Could you give me any notion of the subject of the book?" Sabina hesitated.

"Ah, there you are!" cried William. "And likewise, there you are again! The name Pater," he continued, steering away from dangerous ground, "this author took because it means Father. I know that as a fact. Pater means Father in Latin, just as Mater means Mother."

He astonished himself. He wished his aunt could hear him: he wished all Palebrook could hear him. He was getting to like his part. And there could be no doubt in the world about the intense respect which now shone in Sabina's eyes. ...

"I had no idea your nephew was so learned," he had the satisfaction of hearing her say during the evening. "We've been talking of such profound subjects. He knows Latin and heaps of things."

"Dear me, didn't you know that?" Aunt Laura raised her eyebrows lazily. "I believe he is a poet too, Sabina."

"What on earth possessed you to say I was a poet?" William inquired angrily when he caught her alone. "Haven't I enough to do to keep up the philosopher dodge? You don't want me to have brain fever, do you?"

"Oh, I'm so sorry!" His accomplice laughed idly. "I ought to have said 'philosopher' instead of 'poet.' Now we must stick to it."

Chapter VI

THOUGH WILLIAM MIGHT NOT be a professed philosopher, though he had not, in truth, a spoonful of scholastic philosophy anywhere about him, he yet found himself engaged on a subject of meditation which has occupied no small number of them, to wit: The cruelty and irresponsibility of women. Here was that woman, his aunt, machining with a light hand the most daring schemes, engaging him gaily to the most onerous burthens, and then absconding out of all danger, leaving him to half-kill himself to satisfy her engagements.

It was poetry now. The sun was shining in a sky of tender blue through which little fleecy clouds went spinning; it was a matchless day for sailing, for tennis, for just loafing. But it was poetry now, alas! And with rage in his heart, William attacked for about the fiftieth time the "Laus Veneris," applying his stubborn memory to retain words devoid of sense. It is said that certain pupils have been known to learn propositions of Euclid by heart to such a point that when it comes to demonstrating, if the letters of the figure be changed, they are at once unhorsed; and William was pursuing an analogous mental process. Luckily, his memory was a good one, and had been to a certain extent exercised by cricket scores and at Ibed's.

It was twelve o'clock. His aunt came in, cool and fresh-looking as ever. "What a lovely day! Everybody is out." She sat herself on the arm of a chair and scrutinized her flushed and dishevelled nephew. "Well, how are you getting on?"

It was too much. "It's all right for you," he burst out. "You wouldn't care about it yourself. What would you think of being up against that"—and he thumped the *Poems and Ballads*—"since breakfast?"

"Dear me!" cooed his aunt. "I'm sure I sympathize with you. You look as if you had been working hard. Would you like some beef-tea?"

"Yes, I would." He took five or six leaves of the book between his thumb and forefinger and held the book towards her. "That!" he said significantly. He seemed to be moved by a slight frenzy.

Aunt Laura was impressed. "Good Heavens! don't overstrain yourself whatever you do. I'll have the beef-tea sent up at once. I had no idea," she continued, "that poetry was as hard as that. I thought it was—oh, you know—comic opera and that sort of thing."

"The comic has been left out of this opera," said William bitterly. He drummed moodily on the book. "You wouldn't like to hear me recite, I suppose?" he asked in a tone of injury.

"Oh, of all things!" she clasped her hands fervently. "Do recite something, William."

"I may as well do it before you," he went on rather ungraciously, "because I'll have to do it some time, and I'll be better for practice. I've taken this piece from another of those books." He pointed to a small volume.

And he began:

"*Three fishers went sailing away to the West,*
  Away to the West as the sun went down;
Each thought on the woman who loved him the best,
  And the children stood watching them out of the town."

He worked through the poem, shouting, making what he considered appropriate gestures as he went. Memories of music-hall reciters aided him: he paused at the end of every stanza and deepened his voice. Aunt Laura, with her head on one side, her lips parted, watched him, full of admiration.

"Really, William, you're simply splendid. You're too thrilling for words. You know there's a song something like that. I'm sure I've heard it somewhere."

She said this lightly, not thinking it made any difference. Her notion of the way poetry is produced was vague. If she had been forced to give an opinion, she would have said that she supposed it was got out of other books. It never occurred to her that a poem was the special property of any one poet. This will only shock intellectual circles and culture-clubs; there are really any number of people up and down the world like her. She was the kind of person who attributes the play to the actors, and who can never tell the name of the author of a novel she has been reading. The similarity between what William had just recited and a song she hardly remembered struck her as an amusing coincidence—nothing more, and that was why she mentioned it.

But William saw much farther than that: he was a conscious plagiary. "Then I'll have to chuck it," he said desperately. "There's a morning's work gone to pot. I picked it out because it was seasidey and appropriate. Now it's no use."

"I'm really grieved, William," moaned his aunt, wishing she had kept quiet. "And you've turned out so intellectual and clever too, dear. Does it make so much difference?"

"Oh, it's not your fault, I suppose," William grumbled like a generous martyr. "But I can't very well trot out stale stuff, can I? Sabina would spot it at once." He turned to his table again wearily. "Well, more work. Look here, Aunt Laura, I'd like that beef-tea, please, as soon as it's convenient. This sort of thing makes you hungry. I'll bet any odds you like that I've got some stuff here"—and he slapped his hand down on *Poems and Ballads*—"that you've never heard anyone sing out of an asylum."

Compensation awaited him at lunch in the shape of Sabina's reverent manner. She listened whenever the philosopher and poet spoke as if she were at a solemn service in church. He was wise enough not to speak often. He was on his aunt's left hand, and whenever she thought he was breaking away from his personage she kicked him on the leg. Uncle Herbert, too, had been evidently schooled, and looked on a little mystified, trying to think how the uncle of a great man should act.

Afterwards, out on the lawn, William was lounging and smoking, pretending to read, when Sabina came and sat near him, or rather over against him—it was really as if he were a public building or a statue in a museum—with a piece of embroidery work in her hand. She did not speak: no doubt she feared to disturb his high meditations and was waiting to be spoken to. Through half-closed lids he contemplated her. Even to the most fatuous there was nothing in her attitude to betoken love; but there was an interest and respect which denoted that she must regard the young man sprawling there as an intellectual giant. Aunt Laura had evidently given it to her strong. Enlightened by the hint from his aunt, he was quite shrewd enough to see that this admiration of intellectual effort and the arts was not native in Sabina; it was not even a personal impulse, but the suggestion of a friend—Effie Patten of Newnham College—whom she adored. Neither had it lasted for long: she could hardly be very well up in her subjects. He thought that under these circumstances he would be particularly dull if he could not impress her. She did not love him yet, of course, but it would go hard, since she was in such excellent dispositions, if he could not make her love him. As for his love for her—well, that would take care of itself. With Sabina's four thousand pounds a year jingling in his pocket, he could go and take Ibed by the nose at the head of his clerks.

Other thoughts, less comfortable, assailed him. He brushed them away. "That would somehow work out all right." The bees droned by; the flowers swooned languorously in the warm afternoon; butterflies, splendidly gaudy, dandered over the grass; the old sundial, ivy-clad, cast a long shadow; in the tree near by a thrush was singing, and Sabina in her chair became a pink blur. ...

"Mr. Spring—I hope I don't interrupt your thoughts—but I wonder would you mind writing in my album?"

It was Sabina speaking timidly as she held out the pretty book.

"I have a number of rather well-known people. Members of Parliament whom father has helped, and all that. I always make him take my book when he is presiding at a big meeting. I have several Cabinet Ministers. I have also a number of people we met on the steamer when we went out to New York. See, here is the great woman novelist who wrote 'Symphonies in Slush' for the magazines, and over here is one of the great leaders of the Woman Suffrage movement. But I forgot; you are not on our side in that." She hesitated, blushing a little. "I have no poet, and so I thought——"

It was touching. In an age when the poet has been relegated among English-speaking people to the position of the palmist and the "beauty specialist" in the popular esteem, this thrill of veneration, swelling up in a heart nurtured in commercialdom, for the singing-man, the creator of unpractical ideals, the pursuer of unprofitable loveliness, was something to the credit of our general humanity. For bear in mind that her sentiment was in no way implicated with any attraction to the person of the youth before her; what she gave was a pure tribute, rendered to a man born with a gift which segregated him from the herd of mortals. William himself saw this well enough, but he felt no shame; on the contrary, he considered that what admiration she had to spare he had fairly earned.

"I'll take the book into the house and find a pen and ink," he said, with a rising sense of importance. This was to be a man indeed! But he wished it had been for something which enrolled his sympathies more than poetry.

Sabina, however, had come all prepared. "Perhaps this might do?" and she held out a little gold fountain-pen.

"Capitally." He wrote his name in neat letters: "William Parkman Montagu Spring."

She was looking over his shoulder.

"How many names you have!"

"Family names," said William. Then, with his irresistible tendency to bounce, he added consequentially: "My mother was one of the Montagus."

It occurred to Sabina, who had nothing to learn about social values, that they were a rather extended and variegated clan, stretching from the peerage to the moneylender and second-hand clothes dealer; but she did not make any attempt to locate William's kindred. Who he was interested her not at all; she was only concerned with what he was.

"Perhaps you will read some of your poems one day?" she ventured after a moment.

He had expected this. "One day—oh, yes. I'm getting up some things. They'll be ready shortly."

They had to be ready sooner than he anticipated. The very next morning his aunt came into his room.

"The Parrys have asked us all for to-night. It will be a large party. They hope you will recite some of your poems."

He turned pale. "They hope I'll recite——"

"Yes. I'm afraid you are going to mind, William, but Miss Parry sent that message by Sabina."

"Well, if you haven't got me into a hole! My God, if you haven't got me into a hole!" He lost control of himself altogether. "Look here, do you mean to say I'll have to get up and spout before a room full of people?"

"I'm afraid so," she said, toying with a flower in her belt.

"Well, I won't, my friend. You can risk your little savings on that with perfect safety. I say, with—perfect—safety. I'll go back to London first."

"Ibed's!" murmured Aunt Laura, looking out of the window.

This word, as usual, acted as a cold douche. William tramped about and shoved things here and there as men do when they are in a rage and know they must yield. "How on earth did they know I was a poet?" he asked sullenly at length.

"Sabina, of course. You don't expect she would keep a thing like that quiet? Why, she's proud of it."

"Is she? And do you mean to say that the whole shop knows I'm a poet?"

"I'm afraid so," said Aunt Laura again.

"Well, it's a shame," he cried, breaking down. "I say, it's a shame. My whole holiday is spoiled. Nobody will ask me to anything while I've got that reputation. Who wants a poet moping around? People will think I'm no good at games, and lost in my thoughts, and all that bosh. You never see a poet on the stage that he's not made fun of. I've lost my coat-room check at Palebrook, that's all. I didn't mind the joke just for a few days among ourselves, but if it's going to be public property——Why, my God!" he shouted, appalled, "I shall be pointed at in the streets. I'll be thought balmy!"

She felt sorry for him, and came and put her arm round his shoulders. "Try to bear up, William," she purred soothingly. "If you show the white feather now the whole thing is lost. We'll see it through between us if you'll only pull yourself together. After all, it's not so terrible. You recited splendidly yesterday."

"Oh, before you! That's not a mob."

"Well, all I can say is that everything with Sabina depends on to-night. Stephen is giving her a horseback lesson this morning, and you must do something striking to counteract the effect. Try to take a brace, there's a dear boy."

"It's come so suddenly," said William. "That's the main thing I object to." But he began to feel better.

⁂

In the evening she arranged that she would take William by herself in the carriage, and sent Mr. Burger ahead with Sabina. As soon as they were gone, she called her nephew into the dining-room.

"Well, are you ready? Come here and let me see how you look."

She glanced over the tall, thin young man, and on the whole felt satisfied. He was too tall, his nose was too long, his eyes too small, his feet too big; he had an expression of assurance which might annoy some people; but on the other side, he had thick fair hair, he was fresh-coloured, and he was healthy. Altogether, she thought he looked very nice. She straightened his tie, put a flower in his coat, patted him here and there.

"Oh, stop it, Aunt Laura! You're making me more nervous than I am already."

"I want you to make a good impression." She went to the table and poured out a glass of champagne. "You had better drink this," she said. "It will rouse the lion in you."

"You are sure you know your pieces?" she asked when they were in the carriage.

"What do you think?" At present he was feeling rather lively. "Anyhow, I've got them all written out in case of accident."

"How clever of you to hit upon that!"

"Yes. Now, look here. While I'm spouting, you're not to look at me. You're to keep your head turned away. Do you understand?"

"All right," she laughed. "I'll study my toes. And now let me give you a tip: Don't talk much, and look as serious as you can."

Chapter VII

THE COMPANY ASSEMBLED IN the high rooms of Mr. Parry's Georgian house, many of whom had never seen William, felt at liberty to scrutinize him without concealment. His reputation had pre-ceded him; they had heard a poet would be on view; but they had no formed idea of what poets were like. He might resemble anything, from the cloaked and slouch-hatted villain of the stage, to the poor idiot who on fine days sat sunning on the quay. What they were not prepared for was the ordinary—someone like themselves; and many looking at William—the girls who had speculated vaguely; the young men who had cut the jokes of comic writers about poets; the elders for whom a poet ranked with the organ-grinder and the billiard-marker—felt a trifle disappointed. They were only not absolutely revolted, saved from an unholy sensation that a trick had been put upon them, by the sight of William's pallor, his corrugated brow, a general air of defiance in his bearing.

The truth is that the young man felt he was in the position of an advertised fool. In him the characteristic which could be constantly relied upon was his eagerness to secure the applause of people whose judgments he thought counted, and among these he numbered the society of Palebrook and the country round about. Whatever free airs he might assume, there was always working in him an eager reference to the opinions of such people and an abject fear of their criticism. His dignity lay prone at a mocking smile; his serenity was at the mercy of a whisper; and the assurance of his carriage could be marred by the raising of an eyebrow. No greater sting could have been devised for his vanity than to introduce him thus publicly in the melancholy and contemptible character of a poet, which isolated him as completely from his surroundings as the clown in the circus-ring is isolated from the spectators. No character was more remote from the kind of men he admired than the character of a poet. If he had been asked to choose between coming as a nigger-minstrel or a poet, he would have chosen the former with infinite gusto. Or a boxer, or a step-dancer, or a jockey! Those were occupations which people respected. But a poet! ...

No wonder he looked haggard. It was impossible for him to mix in, to feel at ease, because everybody who spoke to him spoke, as it were, on stilts. If he drew near a group, the laughter hushed. Girls said to him gravely that they supposed he found them too frivolous. The elders were even more insupportable. They patronized him as they might patronize some youth who is not what is called "all there."

"Well, Mr. Spring," sang out old Parry, as the young man wandered disconsolately into the card room. "Mooning, I suppose—always mooning! What fellows you poets are!"

That is a specimen of what he had to bear. Sabina came to him now and then, but her visits, he felt, were inspired by respect, by duty, and she would soon move away again to Ruggles, with whom she seemed to be perfectly happy. William had never liked Ruggles since the day he first met him; what he felt now was hatred. What did a man of that age want at an evening party? If he came, why didn't he stay with the old men and women? Why wasn't he married? Why should he monopolize all the young women, who were probably laughing at him—though as William tried to think this he had an abominable conviction that they were really laughing with the lawyer and perhaps at him—William— the poet—the jay! It was all on account of Ruggles' money, of course:

nobody would tolerate him if he wasn't rich. And this was the man regarded as a rival for Sabina by Aunt Laura!

His aunt, meanwhile, had deserted him completely, and with suppressed fury he watched her, florid and bland, talking and laughing without apparent concern at the other side of the room. He would make her pay for that! More than once he was assailed by a temptation to cut the whole show and go home; it was only the thought of distant Ibed's which helped him to stand his ground. And he had to do some standing, for eleven o'clock had struck before Miss Parry asked him to perform.

All the guests gathered round in varying moods, with barefaced curiosity obviously on top. William, standing, saw his uncle looking at him with an odd mixture of encouragement and pity, and on the fringe of the crowd he caught sight of his aunt's well-dressed head bent down. She had remembered that then! Then all the faces confronting him seemed to blend, except one which stood out oddly: it was the face of a man he had never seen before and never saw after. He passed his hand across his fevered brow, a natural, necessary gesture which was, however, condemned as an affectation.

> *"Asleep or waking is it? for her neck*
> *Kissed over close, wears yet a purple speck*
> *Wherein the pained blood falters and goes out;*
> *Soft, and stung softly—fairer for a fleck."*

He rolled out the great music in a strong voice, and his inflections would have told a listener familiar with verse that he attached little meaning to the words. Shrinking from the labour of learning all the long poem, he had chosen the stanzas at haphazard; and this still more darkened the meaning for the audience, none too expert, as it was, in following poetry.

> *"Ah, yet would God this flesh of mine might be*
> *Where air might wash and long leaves cover me,*
> *Where tides of grass break into foam of flowers,*
> *Or where the wind's feet shine along the sea."*

For all their preventions, their scoffings at poets and poetry, there was not a person in the room, except deaf old cousin Parry, who was not moved by the exquisite periods; so true is it that there is something in the nature of man which responds to poetry, as it responds to a fine day, and that there are chords, rusty from disuse, deep in the breasts of the most earthy which poetry and music can still make vibrate momentarily, faintly, like the strings of an old, old harpsichord whose heart died ages ago and lies buried in dust.

> *"I seal myself upon thee with my might,*
> *Abiding alway out of all men's sight*
> *Until God loosen over sea and land*
> *The thunder of the trumpets of the night."*

… It was finished. There was a slight pause as William sat down, mopping his brow, and then a murmur of admiration. How clever! The women with moist eyes and lips crowded round this young man who could think of such wonderful things, who must have so much passion, so much feeling! And the men too looked on him with a new respect when they thought of the difficulty of tagging all those rhymes, a form of skill which they were open-minded enough to put almost on a level with bringing down a rocketing pheasant. He had had to wait; the time had been sore and long; but now was his hour of triumph. Sabina's eyes shone as she stood before him. Aunt Laura, flushed and handsome, looked as one celebrating the successful outcome of a doubtful scheme. On all sides were congratulations. Questions poured in. Did it take him long to compose it? Had he anything else ready? Oh yes; it was his hour of triumph.

That is to say, with all but one. Stephen Ruggles stood a little apart, perplexed.

> *"Until God loosen over sea and land*
> *The thunder of the trumpets of the night."*

Where had he heard that before? That he had heard it before was certain. Not that he had a wider knowledge of verse than anyone else in the room. It might even be said that he had less. Two or three were there who had read the Church hymns out of church; *The Christian Year*; possibly a little Longfellow. In a community whose reading wants were sufficiently supplied by some middle-aged novels provided by a badly oiled lending library at the druggist's, he was, in this matter at all events, not exceptional. At Palebrook the classical British poets were as little known as they are, I suppose, in Nigeria. If the prose-writers had few acquaintances, how should the poets be recognized? It is hardly necessary to add that this infrequentation of the classics was in no wise incompatible with the fact that the town boasted of two ladies and a gentleman who contributed occasionally to the magazines. Indeed, one of these ladies, who was among the first to felicitate William, had a story called "Annie's Overshoes" appearing at that moment in an American periodical; and she was wont to declare that she never read anything but contemporary literature from fear of injuring the big-hearted modern outlook which was recognized in her productions by publishers and critics.

But the case of Ruggles was of another kind altogether. He had never written anything except legal papers and private letters, and he had read very few books besides law books. This memory of lingering verse that haunted him was due to an invalid sister, dead now some years, who was fond of reading poetry aloud, to which he used to pretend to listen merely to humour the sick woman, without really paying much attention. Yet those two lines had stuck in his head. He had no acquaintance whatever with poets in the flesh, but the blond, self-satisfied William did not seem to him to suit the part. However little he might know about poetry, he understood at least that the sombre, magnificent stanzas which the young man had just recited as his own were the result of some tremendous effort of an astonishing genius; and to his shrewd eyes, trained to gauge men, William seemed the most ordinary of mortals. Of course there were cases of the baffling exterior, concealing in some measure a man's real powers; but he felt certain that all William was there before his eyes, on the surface. Given stable conditions in that young man's life, and he could predict his career to a certainty. He had seen hundreds like him; not a few had passed through his professional hands.

Still, although he judged William to be the kind of man he did not care about or value, he knew him too little to dislike him. His feelings however in this matter were given a sharper edge than they might otherwise have had by his discovery of the machinations of the Burgers to throw Sabina and her fortune into their nephew's arms, for he had almost made up his mind to marry Sabina himself.

He moved over to where William stood walled by admirers.

"That was a very great poem you gave us," he said in his cold, incisive voice. "If it is your own, I congratulate you."

William gave a surly nod and half turned away. He did not see why he should be civil to Ruggles.

"The reason I say that," pursued the other, "is because there are some lines in it which remind me of a poem I know already."

This was too much! William's eyes blazed. What! After his untold labours, was he to be robbed of his gains in the very moment of triumph by this six-and-eightpenny blighter? He glanced over Ruggles, noted the well-brushed hair, and the evident attention to details of dress.

"Oh indeed! Is there anything about an old buck in it?" he asked as offensively as he could.

"Or about an old maid?" cried the delightful voice of Aunt Laura, who feared a storm.

Ruggles had far too much usage of the County Court not to have perfect control of his temper. He went on musing as if the other had not spoken.

"It's very singular. I know the lines, but I can't for the life of me remember the poem or the author."

"Oh, that's very likely," William sneered. "I've always heard that as we get old things don't come back to us quite so easily."

And he walked off to supper. He was now become such a personage that several of the younger guests, especially the girls, thought his reply extremely witty. Among the elderly it was not quite so much relished: they felt it reflected a little on themselves. One of these came up and took the poet affectionately by the arm. It was old Smalt, the vicar.

"Now you mustn't be too hard on us oldsters, my boy," said he, looking at the youth in his odd way. "I'm old—sixty-seven—but I like youth myself. You have a great head."

Miss Pick, the aforementioned author of "Annie's Overshoes," chimed in:

"And so modern! Nothing like that could have been written except in this century—I may say, in the last five years since Marinetti revealed us to ourselves."

"Hum!" said the vicar. "Marinetti, did you say? I take it he is an Italian. I only know Italy B.C. Don't you ever read the old authors, Miss Pick?"

"Never!" replied Miss Pick proudly. "That is, I believe I once just glanced at Fielding and Defoe and those sort of people, but they are so irredeemably sordid and squalid. Quite out of date. Men want sunshine."

"And babies want pap," snapped old Smalt who liked to do the preaching himself. He turned again to William. "You have a splendid sense of rhythm, language, and so on. I never read anything myself except the Latin authors, theology, and the *Times;* but I'll buy a copy of your poems any day you like. And a word in your ear." He drew closer to him. "Never mention marriage in your love-poems by way of making them respectable. Whatever else poetry should be, it should never be respectable." And with that he went off chuckling.

"Old beast!" thought William, distressfully. "I wonder how many more of them I'll have to stand."

Watchful Aunt Laura saw he was unnerved, and gathering up her Throgmorton and Sabina, made a move for home. When they got there, Sabina, who was generally so still and undemonstrative, ran up to William with enthusiasm.

"Mr. Spring, I want to tell you I never heard anything so noble. I didn't quite follow it all—Miss Pick has just been telling me that modern poetry is not meant to make sense—but the way you spoke was beautiful. I shall hardly be able to sleep for thinking of it. You are a great man."

She was breathless, her eyes were moist, and Aunt Laura thought she detected in her accent something more than respect. In fact, this lady was confident enough, on her way to bed, to give her opinion to her husband that it was a sure thing between William and Sabina.

Chapter VIII

"Until God loosen over sea and land
The thunder of the trumpets of the night."

FOR DAYS THE VERSES were in his head—an obsession. Where did they come from?' He was more certain than ever that he had heard them before: the trumpets of the night bellowing out suddenly over the melancholy ocean had left a definite furrow in his memory. Where did the lines come from? He would drop to a halt at corners, fall into a brown study over his meals, start from his sleep thinking he had caught them.

His sister's books had drifted away after her death, but there were a few eighteenth-century poets in the house—old, dust-laden editions of Beattie, Cowper, *The Vanity of Human Wishes*. These he searched patiently line for line: he had hardly realized there was so much poetry in the world. In addition to this stock, all the poetry he was able to borrow in Palebrook was a copy of *Evangeline*, which one of the Ford girls had received as a school prize, and a book of quite recent verse called "Flamingoes" by Miss Pick's brother who belonged to the Futurist school. And yet if he had only the key to those two lines in his hand, he could brain William with it! In a sense, they stood between him and four thousand a year.

This fact, he thought one morning as he journeyed along in the train, was becoming more evident day by day. Since that night of poetry the manner of Sabina had changed a little to him; in Palebrook society, where everybody knew what everybody else was doing, it was currently reported that she was showing an unmistakable preference for William. If Ruggles had been in love with Sabina this report would have made him angry: as he saw in her simply a more or less amiable little woman—amiable, that is to say, when she was feeling well and had not been crossed—who would make an advantageous match, what he took from the Palebrook report was an encouragement to be wary. He had almost too much contempt for William to bear him any malice on the personal score; but he found the youth in his way, and he meant, as he put it, to side-track him once for all. William, he thought, would look rather better when the grass was growing round his arrested wheels.

He left the train at Southampton, where he had a bankruptcy case to look after; and as soon as his work in court was ended he made his way to the large shop of a bookseller and stationer. There he sent in his name to the manager, who presently appeared.

"Good morning, Mr. Malkin. I want you to try to help me. I am looking for a poetry-book which has these lines."

And a little embarrassed for so imperturbable a person, Ruggles, first looking around to see that the shop was empty of customers, started declaiming:

> "Until God loosen over sea and land
> The thunder of the trumpets of the night."

The manager was an excellent man: he took it as a matter of course. He pursed his lips, put his finger to his brow, appeared to consider. Then he shook his head.

"N—no," he said slowly, "no, I can't say I remember them. They sound a little like Tennyson. You wouldn't care to buy a volume of Tennyson and look it through? We have a nice cheap edition."

A young lady standing behind the stationery counter here interposed:

"Excuse me, Mr. Malkin, I can inform you where the lines occur which the gentleman just said. They are in Swinburne's Laws Veneerus. I know much of it by heart."

Ruggles looked at her admiringly. The precision of her diction was reflected by an air of tranquil competence all over her good-looking person. "She's a wonder," thought Ruggles.

"Swinburne!" cried the manager. "Bless me, so they are. How stupid of me not to think of it! We have all Swinburne's works, I think. Just get down the right volume, will you, miss?" And in a moment he presented *Poems and Ballads.* "Nine shillings."

"Nine shillings for a book of poetry!" repeated Ruggles in dismay. His estimation of poetry as a means of acquiring a fortune went up considerably. "However does it sell?"

"Oh, we get it; we get it, I assure you," said the bookseller; while the young lady, taking the volume from the lawyer's hand, opened it at a certain place. And there in cold print was the poem William had recited as his own. It was well worth the money.

"Miss Sacheverel," said the manager, as soon as Ruggles had gone out of the shop, "you must leave the stationery and fancy goods after to-morrow and go into the book department. And I'll see about raising your salary."

As for Ruggles, seated in the train on his way home, while others around him read the sporting papers, the fashion papers, or the novel cheap and light, like the claret provided by certain wine-merchants, he read the "Laus Veneris." Then he closed his book and set his fancy volving and revolving by what device he would blast William in Palebrook. He had him there to squeeze between the covers of the book, but he must contrive to do it cleanly. It would not be to his interest, nor had he the least desire, to mortify the Burgers through their nephew. All he wanted was to sweep the youth definitely out of Sabina's way, and incidentally to make him smart in the process. Sabina in her new-found enthusiasm for the arts, was attracted by the poet: expose the sham, and William must became as good as dead to her, for she did not care for William himself.

So he reasoned, planning out his game at his ease as a player who holds most of the trumps scans smilingly his hand, or as your boxer who has got his man well licked postpones the blow which will give him his quietus from mere pleasure in exercising his science. Sometimes both of them are beaten, with the very taste of victory in their mouths.

Chapter IX

ONE MORNING, WHEN HE had been about two weeks at "The Firs," William, upon coming down to breakfast, found a letter. He knew that writing, based on the standard model, altered by the writing of German, and set off by certain sweeps and flourishes which seemed not spontaneous, but proceeding rather from a desire to write a different hand from other people, to achieve something personal. He tore the envelope hastily. "Dearest Will"; and further down a sentence about Palebrook. "Oh, my God!" He stuffed the letter in his pocket and eyed his breakfast with little of his wonted relish.

Sabina with anxious eyes noted his pallor. William first maintained vehemently that there was nothing the matter; then, driven to find excuses, he muttered about disturbed sleep, bad dreams. Sabina had a picture of the poet wrestling like Jacob with the angel through the watches of the night, and she said aloud, in a tone which expressed more than the words, that the practice of composing poetry must be bad for the health in the long run. Uncle Herbert agreed with her. Privately, he thought that he had nothing to say against the poetry dodge since it had done the business with Sabina, but he was the kind of man who called it all damned skittles. He offered to make his nephew a brandy-cocktail from an excellent prescription given him by the steward of an American yacht. "It will buck you up like half-past six." William could hear the groaning of his heart.

As soon as he was able, he hastened to a retired corner of the grounds, and with a stiff face began reading the letter.

"58 PESHAWUR TERRACE,
July 17, 1914.

"DEAREST WILL,—Why have you not written? Since we had a telegram from you two weeks ago saying you were all right nothing has come, though I have watched the post anxiously every day. Of course I am glad to hear you are all right, but mother thinks you might have asked about us, and also sent your address. As we were getting so anxious about you, fearing you might be ill or something, I went around to your lodgings, and Mrs. Benn told me she had heard from you only yesterday, asking her to forward some things, saying that you thought you wouldn't be coming back to London for some time. She seemed surprised that we did not know where you were. My classes finish to-morrow, thank goodness! and what do you think we have decided to do? We are going to spend our holiday at Palebrook. We have looked it up on the map, and the sea-air will be just the thing to counteract the effects of mother's cigarette-smoking. Besides, mother thinks we should make the acquaintance of your relations. So please look out lodgings for us (mother says, not too dear, but not stuffy, poky little rooms either) and meet us at the station to-morrow afternoon, 5.38. Don't forget. Dear old Will, what good times we shall have. We'll go on a regular bust up!

"Affectionately yrs.,
"PENELOPE HAZARD.

"P.S.—Mother says that in case you cannot find decent lodgings at once, we shall go to the hotel advertised in the A B C for a few days. But it must not be for long. Awful rush for the post.   P. H."

Men who contemplate suicide, it may be surmised, do not hate the even tenor of the world. The sunshine warms their hearts out on the open road far from the haunts of man; here no troubles press; and could this continue all would be well. But they know that night is coming inexorably on, and with the night, hands to pluck at them out of the darkness. Since William had come into the country and fallen to work out his aunt's plan for his advancement, he had always had Penelope at the back of his head, and entertained her there without uneasiness. As long as she was not at Palebrook, or likely to be, he could contemplate her with equanimity, persuade himself that he intended no change in his relations with her, and place their connection among that number of other things which one lets run on to see how they will turn out. He liked Penelope so; she did not bother; he had her always to fall back upon.

He had been engaged to her for over a year, though he wore his ligaments easily. He thought he loved her, and he did like her on the whole better than Sabina. During the last few weeks, since he had been much with Sabina, he had sometimes caught himself thinking that it would be brisker with Pen. Not that he had any violent passion for her either; and such passion as there was had stagnated considerably since the day he asked her to marry him—a step he had often since considered rather precipitate, though he remembered it to Pen's credit that since then she had always been willing to lend him money when she had any in hand.

Still, she had shown him some astonishing paces in the way of fickleness, fretfulness, and arbitrary humours. After such agitating experience, he found Sabina a relief, mainly because she was different. She, too, had her moods, and he suspected that she might have her sulks; but he thought it hopeless to find any woman in the world without these incommodities. What pleased him in Sabina, besides the respect she paid him as a genius, was her unassertiveness, her good manners. Pen might have a better manner than Sabina, but Sabina had better manners. You could be certain that Sabina would never make a violent scene, or do any of those other unpleasant things which reveal a temperament. She had, moreover, that indefinable air of sureness and, small as she was, of command, that air of one who never dreams that her orders may be disputed, which accompanies great wealth; and of all this Pen had never a vestige. It takes a good deal of money from the cradle up to make what is called a lady. Then there was of course the money itself, always dangling like a monstrous yellow fruit before his eyes. Still, he thought that he liked Penelope best.

That is, in the distance. At Palebrook she was simply fatal. Far off, she might be taken for the secure wayside under the sun; here, she was the night, and suicidal vision of hands clutching from the darkness. There was no use in trying to put the visitation off: the mother was too indolent to change a plan she had already decided upon, and the daughter would suspect a ruse and come all the faster. Although her letter was evidently written in two moods—it was so like her to change her mood in the space of time it takes to write a letter—it was only too plain from the name signed in full that the mood belligerent predominated. He would have to give up Sabina; he would have to go back and drudge at Ibed's till he had a good enough salary to marry Penelope. Nor will it surprise anyone who has reflected a little on the inconsistency of mankind, that his most poignant regret out of all this was that he would never be in a position to go and swagger before Ibed's clerks.

And all because of the impetuosity of a headstrong girl! Why had she chosen Palebrook to come to? Simply to be devilish. Having nobody to occupy her, to see what she was about, she decided to come and see what he was about. She loved him, he supposed—nay, he believed it thoroughly; but the thought, at other times comfortable to his vanity, was no consolation. She had simply ruined him.

Other visions surged, created by his heat-oppressed brain. He could see Ruggles and the other Palebrookites, but especially Ruggles, nudging and winking when they heard of the engagement. So that was the end of all the poetry and stuff! The heiress would go to Ruggles. From the despair engendered by this thought sprang half a resolution to confide the whole story to his aunt. She was good-natured; she might sympathize with him. After all, there was nothing to be ashamed of in it. But no—he dared not. However good-natured she might be, she would not see her plan brought to ruin with equanimity. She might even blame his deceit—women were so unpractical and ridiculous! She was capable of asking him to pack his bag, and there would be the end of his glory! Still, he would have to tell her something; and he plunged his hands deep in his pockets, frowning down on the common mother and bedfellow of us all with the face of a man whom wanton gods tormented for their sport.

He caught her in the little sitting-room just after lunch. She was writing letters, and turned round cheerfully.

"Come in, William. Have you brought some poetry to try over?"

William felt anything but merry, and when he was in trouble he always lost his off-hand manner, and his naturally harsh voice took on a whining tone, combining the reproach, the grumble, and the apology in about equal quantities—a voice which showed as well as anything else the kind of man he would be later.

"Really, Aunt Laura," he droned, "you never seem to be serious about anything. I never saw anyone like you."

"Oh, William dear, don't do that! It ages you dreadfully. I'll be as serious as you like. What has been broken?"

"Broken? Nothing that I know of. Why should anything be broken? The fact is, Aunt Laura, I had a letter this morning from some friends of mine. They asked me to look them out lodgings in Palebrook."

"Oh, how nice! You had better send them to Mrs. Wrench's in the High Street. She has really good rooms. Her husband used to be one of the servants at Palebrook Court, so he knows all about men's things. I shall be driving by there this afternoon and I'll let the Wrenches know, if you like. What kind of men are they?"

William gulped. "They're not exactly men, Aunt Laura. In fact they're two ladies—a Mrs. Hazard and her daughter. Quite nice people. Mr. Hazard was an architect before he died. I've known them some time. They live near me in London. Mrs. Hazard has two sons, so I go in occasionally of an evening. You get so lonely in lodgings by yourself after a hard day in the City. There are always a good many people there and it passes the time."

Aunt Laura nibbled her pen. "Oh yes," she said slowly. "I see perfectly. But what an extraordinary thing to pick out a little place like Palebrook! However, I hope they'll enjoy it, I'm sure. I'll call, of course, and we'll do what we can to brighten it up for them. Wouldn't they care for the hotel? It is not at all a bad place. Of course it would be dearer than lodgings. But I suppose your friends are fairly well-to-do?"

"Well, they're not paupers, if that's what you mean. They are not millionaires either." Then he thought it advisable to bring out some of the truth. "Penelope Hazard gives lessons in drawing and painting sometimes. She's awfully clever. She's been a lot abroad. You're sure to like her."

He was overdoing it.

Aunt Laura mused again, staring at her desk. "Yes; I see it all from here. They will find it very nice at the Wrenches' and not at all expensive. Penelope, did you say? What a pretty name! She's not married or anything like that?" she asked, looking up.

"No," replied William. "Not that I know of."

"Oh. And she is pretty?"

"Well, not what you call——" His headshake was depreciating.

The Second Part

Mendelssohn–Chopin Development

Chapter X

No, NOT PRETTY, SHE decided, as she came away after her visit—
not at all pretty. The girl was something less than that; she was
also considerably more. Judged by the Palebrook standard of beauty
she was deficient. Put her beside Jessie Bartlet, Vera Ford, or the other
recognized beauties of the neighbourhood—broad-shouldered, firm,
well-moulded, strong, with the vivid complexions of perfect health—
and there was not a man thereabouts who would have preferred her.
But Aunt Laura's perceptions were not organically provincial, and it
occurred to her that in some sophisticated, tense societies, where people lived on their nerves, where the senses were rather jaded, where the
perceptions were so sharpened that only the exotic, the out-of-the-way,
could rouse any interest—well, among such people, Pen's languid mor-
tal charm, so remote from acknowledged types, with her unfathom-
able, even dimly treacherous smile, might stir the deadliest passions.
Such strange poisonous beauty as arises from a lone miasmal tarn lying
blood-shot under a westering sun, or from some monstrous pharma-
ceutical garden where the plants in the twilight breathe forth odours so
heavy that the soul of one who walks therein is torn with sobs; aspects
of the night of fire, of bloody flagellations, of a cruelty that ever smiles,
and of the chamber of death—all, all could be seen, by one who had
eyes to see, in Pen's wan countenance and lithe, panther-like grace.

Aunt Laura had her limitations of vision, but in certain atmospheres
she could see much farther than many people in Hampshire, or possibly in other counties. And watching Pen as she stood before her, tall
and fragile, a veritable tower of ivory, in Mrs. Wrench's low-ceilinged
parlour, she felt, with an odd seizure not altogether pleasant, that here
was in the flesh one of those dangerous women whom one reads or
hears about but never meets—one of those women who spread anger
and quarrel and lamentation, often disaster and ruin, where they pass.
Such as this was she under whose kiss King Solomon died to pleasure,
and such as this she who watched with inscrutable eyes the ships drifting into Troy and the pinnacles of Ilium burning. To love her not at all
were possible and easy; but he who did love her would be drunk with
love; and to feel her lips clinging to his, her amber hair brushing his
face, and her long arms about his neck, would sink to the nether end of
Hell content. ...

All this Aunt Laura stated to herself in her own terms, of course, of the worldly-wise woman, but with immense conviction. She was trying to be fair about it, for Pen was not the kind of person that she herself liked, although she acknowledged that many women might like her. She thought her too tall and too thin; the abstract lines of her face were ordinary, and her colour too wan. The mouth looked peevish, dissatisfied, even bitter at times, and the curved nose narrowed in profile all the other features. Her abrupt disconnected manner revealed that she was at the mercy of her impulses, and those not very stable ones. A little petulant, a little defiant, and withal a little timid, she gave the general impression of one who was rather badly treated. The serene lady who was discreetly studying her while she chatted about Palebrook, suspected that storms of hysterical temper often swept over that face, followed by long fits of brooding and dolorous tears. And how old was she?

Pen had gone out of the room to get some music, and her mother replied that she was twenty-five. Aunt Laura said she looked younger, and thought she looked older. Now that she knew her age, she fancied that Pen suffered from indigestion and neurasthenia, and that when she woke in the morning her nose would be reddish. Few unmarried girls arrived at that age with equable tempers and perfect digestions unless they developed grave interests in life, or exercised themselves continually at open-air sports; and Pen did not look as if she did either. The obsession of the future husband, never at rest in girls such as Pen, was unnerving; and even when he did turn up, the long engagement was demoralizing, and made for anaemia, moods, sourness. But she acknowledged, when Pen at a certain moment looked at her full in the face, that she possibly exaggerated the ill-natured side of the girl's character, for she had hitherto failed to take note of the soft eyes, wherein there lurked a kind of latent and continual reproach. ...

"The mother is a cypher," she said to Sabina, to whom she was giving an off-hand account of these friends of her nephew.

She had, in fact, without showing the least curiosity, found out all she wanted to know. These were people who revealed themselves with a little encouragement. Aunt Laura was in possession of the small house in Peshawur Terrace, the occasional difficulties with tradesmen, the lessons Pen gave, and hated to give, in drawing, painting, and languages. The mother was there, flaccid, fatigued-looking, meagre, will-less, turning to her daughter for support whenever she went so far as to assert anything. With plenty of money and no worries she might still have had a certain attraction; but the sordid grind of narrow means in London had taken the life out of her. She was dressed in some hot-looking black stuff, spectacles bridged her nose, and she wore a "false front" which left no room for illusion. Beneath it her forehead showed dry and seamed. And from what she heard, the visitor concluded that when the poor woman was not tyrannized over by her daughter, she was bullied by her two sons, one a lawyer's clerk, and the other in the employ of an omnibus company.

"Mother smokes too much, I'm afraid," said Penelope. "Do you smoke?"

Aunt Laura smiled. "We haven't yet got beyond doing that in secret at Palebrook."

"Really?" Pen glided on. "How funny to make a secret of it! Why, in Spain, where I was for two years, so many women smoke. La Marquesa de Donadio smokes as much as mother. I have seen a great deal of Europe. I was two years in Munich, two years in Brussels, and two years in Madrid for the languages. And I went about a lot, you know."

Aunt Laura knew that she herself had a beautiful speaking voice—a gift she had long been aware she was the sole possessor of among her acquaintance. But here in Pen she found she had a rival. Pen's voice was as exquisite an instrument in its way as her own; but it was utterly different. It was rather disconsolate. It was hesitating, wavering, due perhaps to the Tower of Babel she carried in her head. It was low, sinking often almost to a whisper, and it flowed on like the cooing of doves on summer noons, or again like the plashing of a brook in lone places, or like the wind in fir-trees on a still day. Tired, broken, a little chanting, it slowed down fatigued at the end of each phrase. ...

"My children tell me I have every vice," said Mrs. Hazard with a feeble smile. "Pen, dear, do play something. You play so well."

... "And then I came away," said Aunt Laura to Sabina, who seemed curious. "The girl is very graceful, but I think you will find she doesn't make the most of herself. When one is so peculiarly tall and thin one should have some peculiarities in dress. She dresses like all the world— all the world that don't know how to dress themselves. Her playing is just so-so—*pension* playing."

"Does she play better than me?" asked Sabina.

"My dear!—there is no comparison," cried Aunt Laura adroitly, and left Sabina to pocket the compliment.

Chapter XI

As soon as the visitor was gone, Pen ran up to her bedroom and proceeded to wash her hair. Then she stood before the little square of mirror, shaking out the thick coils of amber-coloured hair which streamed down over her bare arms and shoulders.

"I wish I was dead," she thought.

She looked around the little bedroom, sparsely and cheaply furnished, disgustfully. The bed was an iron cot without tester or valance, covered with a coarse, parti-coloured quilt. A much-used carpet was spread over the middle of the floor, and at the sides the boards were polished. Two flimsy yellow cane-bottomed chairs, a wooden washstand painted yellow, the dressing-table with Pen's brushes and manicure-case and bottles upon it: that was about all. A cheap lace curtain fluttered before the little window. The humble trophies of Mrs. Wrench's taste on the wall, texts in narrow gilt frames for the most part, roused the girl's scorn. "Remember thy Creator in the days of thy youth," was one of them.

"That would be a good joke if an old woman of eighty took the room."

She smiled at herself in the glass, and this reminded her to spread out her lips and inspect her small even teeth. And her thoughts ran on.

"I wonder how much longer this is going to last. I have no luck. I suppose I must go on teaching, teaching to the end of the chapter. I see nothing else. I hate teaching. I loathe and detest poverty. I should like heaps of money to buy all the dresses and jewels I want. I've only got a few rotten little things. Perhaps I might have done better if I had agreed to what Luis proposed in Spain. I'm sure he loved me. He was jolly well worked up. But then there was his wife. It would have been a sin, I suppose. Still, if you think like that you never get anything. The heaps of presents I might have had if I had only——. I should like to have all the money that woman has who was here just now. William's aunt. She's awfully rich. But William won't get any of it. If I marry William it will be just the same old grind, only worse, in a filthy little house where the smell of the dinner cooking knocks you down when you open the front door. I suppose I must marry William. I suppose I'm fond of him. He didn't seem any too anxious to see me. He's up in a big house, with heaps of servants, enjoying himself now, and I'm in a lodging. Heigh-ho! Never mind."

She shifted a little, put her elbows on the table and rested her chin in her hands—her long thin hands, fragile and morbid as the hands of saints and princesses who fold them naïvely in old church windows. And staring at her face in the glass, aureoled with that cloak of amber-coloured hair which seemed as if powdered with dark gold, she continued her incoherent meditations. They were the etchings of her awkward character, which no adequate steering-gear governed: of its unexpected jerks forward and bolts at furious speed; its vertiginous twists, turns; and then, sudden arrest, followed often by wreckage. She oscillated between the song-and-dance theatre and the Methodist chapel, and lately she had thought much of turning Roman Catholic, though she knew little or nothing of this religion. But among her pupils were one or two in convent schools, and she had with them sometimes attended the services, finding that the gloom, the lights, the mysterious vested priests, the scent of incense and flowers, and the long white chants—the very cry of yearning of the soul, of her soul, from the undefined to the unseen—stirred in her corresponding harmonies. After all that, she would go home saying to herself (unless she had somebody by her to say it to): "I am going to be really good, I am going to think of nothing but my salvation"; and she would sit for an hour frowning over the *Vie Dévote* of St. Francis de Sales which a nun had lent her.

But those who were most in her company saw that the main result of all this religiosity showed in extraordinary outbreaks of perversity, in which she tortured herself, tortured others, with the subtle devisements of the sufferer from hysteria. As she thought her health much worse than it was, and as she was, in fact, not seldom undone by her nerves, the fear of Hell had many a chance to sound its lurid note, creating the fiercest discords with the music of the mount of Venus by which she was often ravished. That was her native air, and she would have been happy if she could have allowed herself to breathe it freely. Love in a gold frame, a splendid excitement, high revel untarnished by the sense of sin, of remorse—that is the way her nature, unwarped, uncompressed, would have worked itself out. But during her girlhood her father had gone from loose Anglicanism to strict Wesleyanism, tinctured with gloomy mysticism; and each of his changes had reverberated in her impressionable soul. The consequence was that her body was ever agitated by wrestling bouts between her nature and training, neither of which she was absolutely for or against. No decided choice was on her face; both dispositions showed there at different times and it was impossible to tell from her looks which was strongest; she might be a nun turned rake or a rake turned nun. And so this wave of religiosity having twisted instead of remoulding her nature, it may well be said that it had spoiled her and was the cause of her worst caprices. Hers was one of those spirits, the despair of all guides to the spiritual life, for whom religion, breaking out sporadically, in sudden squalls, in fierce emotional spells, and as suddenly subsiding, is no benefit, but rather a poison.

It was, she remembered, during one of these spells at Munich, coming home from the Maundy Thursday service at the Frauenkirche, all her nerves saturated with flowers, and white vestments, and organ music, and the sympathetic devotion of a great crowd, that she suddenly rounded on a German lieutenant whom she had hitherto encouraged to the utmost, accused him publicly of insulting her, and embroiled him with his family. When she thought over this episode now she considered it rather bad style. It was rather too like the adventuresses who frequent *table-d'hôtes*. She remembered him with his strong face and blue eyes so full of love for her—that desperate love impossible to mistake—and wondered where he was.

"He ought to have proposed to me and I would have married him. He was the nicest man I ever met; and as for brains, the others are fools to him."

Most likely he would have done so if she had not smashed the matter so suddenly. Why had she? What possessed her? Well, Frida had been scoffing about the lengths English girls would go in flirting; and then she felt so good that day coming from church, and the lieutenant had chosen his moment badly to look at her with yearning eyes. And oh!—altogether it was something of which she could never render a satisfactory account to herself, though she had defended herself again and again to others; something over which she had not complete control, which she would not do if it were to do again.

The air, rippling through the window ajar, puffed out the curtain, and a brush fell on the floor. She picked it up and flung it across the room.

"Damn you! Blast you!"

Then she called herself an idiot, and decided to go downstairs and blow off steam on her mother. She felt a need to do that. If there was one thing about her more remarkable than another, it was that she had no inner life. Never was any one less self-contained. All the windows of her soul she tossed up, flung the furniture out of doors, and summoned the passengers to look on. Nor had this anything to do with frankness, unless there be frankness in a leaky bucket. She was not in the least frank: her mode of action was often oblique; she gave the impression, in fact, that everyday intercourse with her was rather unsafe. Her expansiveness was simply an irrepressible need to have others troubling about what troubled her. Sages have found that the best sauce to some things is discretion, and the enclosed garden has enticed many. Pen's garden was common land trampled over by a thousand alien feet that she invited within the palings. Her mother was in possession of the minutest details of her love affairs—not only her mother. She told them to her brothers, to her friends, to anybody with whom she grew a little familiar.

She slipped on a terra-cotta dressing-gown and plaited her hair in two long coils. Possibly from her frequentation of convents, she had acquired a little of the look of the nun when she was standing preoccupied, a little of the nun's demureness and pensiveness, and her hands fell together below her waist nun-like. As she stood a moment thus, with her well-moulded neck bare and her pale head delicately poised upon it, she seemed like one of those tall lilies sick of their virginity which deck the altars of churches on festivals. ...

She found her mother smoking a cigarette and reading *What Every Woman Ought to Know*—Mrs. Hazard's sole occupations, save checking tradesmen's bills when she was at home. Pen took a cigarette and sat down with her elbows on her knees, staring at the grate. She was in her blackest mood; and her mother, who was afraid of her, and whom dire experience had made weather-wise, forbore to speak.

After about a quarter of an hour Pen looked up. "Did you like that woman who was here this afternoon?"

"Yes, dear, I thought she was very nice."

Pen bounded. "Oh, you think everybody is very nice. You can't see through people at all. I hated her. She came here simply to examine us—anyone could see that. There was no nice feeling about it. You could see she knew we were poor and she was patronizing us all the time. And when you think that I'm engaged to her nephew! I call it insolent. I vote we don't call."

"But she doesn't know about the engagement," put in the mother.

"Simply because William said it would be better if he explained it himself. I'm sorry I agreed to that now. It seems low. After all, I'm not so anxious to marry her nephew. It's no honour for us. We're as good as all the Springs and Burgers that ever existed. These people have got more money, that's all. If they hadn't money they would be nothing. Father's father was a Lord Mayor, wasn't he? Why didn't you bring that out to her?"

"I hadn't a chance, my dear. How could I begin talking about Lord Mayors! Besides, I thought you liked her, and I thought you were fond of William. I never know where I am with you."

Pen blew out a long puff of smoke and deliberately picked a shred of tobacco from her lip. "I don't see why not," she said, with concentrated spleen. "I'm above-board enough. As for William, of course I'm fond of him, but I think he's acting like a cad. I don't care whether I marry him or not. We may be engaged, but I don't care. *Je m'en fiche pas mal!*"— she cried this out with amazing vehemence—"*je m'en fiche pas mal!* I never had anything from William except a rotten little ring worth about three pounds. Jack said he was sure it wasn't worth more, and as he's your son, I suppose you'll believe him. I don't know what you want to force me into marrying William for. I think it's most undignified of you. William goes swaggering round like a song and chorus—*Ach Gott!*—and do you know what he really is? He's one of the *à peu près*. Don't you think so?"

"I don't know half what you're talking about. You use so many foreign words. Oh, Pen, you make me so tired. I wish you would give me my cup of cocoa and let me go to bed."

Pen examined the little yellow-labelled tin. "There are only about two spoonfuls left, and I shan't be able to sleep a wink unless I have a cup." Then she relented. "You don't mind, do you, mother dear? You can have it if you like."

The mother made haste to reject the sacrifice.

Pen subsided into a better humour. "I don't mind that woman so much," she said airily. "Did you notice her gown? It looks simple, but it couldn't have cost a penny under fifty pounds. She reminds me rather of that Señora Espantoso at Seville I told you about. She's an awfully rich woman, too, and awfully common. But she's really good fun. She's vulgar, you know, but not in the way that makes you angry. She told me that the day she was married——" Pen launched out on a story, and ended in fits of laughter. "There's nothing bad in that."

"My dear, it's quite bad enough," remonstrated the mother.

Chapter XII

AUNT LAURA WAS HABITUALLY so serene that the least cloud passing across her face was noteworthy.

"Of course," she said, "you will do as you like." Her tone conveyed: "And don't blame me for the consequences."

William was not at all at his ease. "But you can't object to my seeing them since they are here? I must pay them some attention."

"I don't object at all. Far from it. I rather like the Hazards; the daughter seems a nice unhealthy sort of girl. Remember to ask them to come to my party on Friday evening. I have been thinking that your holidays will soon be over, and then you must bid us all good-bye and go back to Ibed's." She paused to let this sink in. "Sabina is having another horseback lesson to-day from Stephen. They seem to be getting very fond of each other's company. Unless you have lost all interest in her, how would it do to give us some more poetry on Friday night? I could bring it in quite naturally."

But William turned pale. "For God's sake, Aunt Laura, don't do that!"

How could he give himself out as a poet before Pen? He saw her listening, supercilious. She was capable of throwing doubts publicly on his claims, out of sheer envy at his attracting more attention than she did.

Aunt Laura took note of his agitation and put it down to the wrong account. "Miss Hazard doesn't strike me as a girl who would make a very useful wife for a poor man," she remarked in a detached tone.

And with that she turned back to the house.

He had not been five minutes in Mrs. Wrench's parlour before he was thinking that Miss Hazard would not make a useful wife for any kind of man, except a professional wife-beater. Pen had on exhibition her special brand of sulks, and sat mute while Mrs. Hazard and William struggled in embarrassed conversation. At last the mother, exhausted, suggested that William should take Pen for a walk. Although the girl heard this proposition, she waited till William had repeated it with an air of spontaneity which came rather tardily off.

"I may as well do that as sit here," she said, rising.

He tried to steer her to the unfrequented quay. She insisted on going through the town, and they encountered the Fords, the Bartlets, the Corders, the Parrys—the whole of Palebrook. For a man and a woman to be strolling together in manifest sulks reveals such a degree of intimacy between them that those who met the pair concluded that young Spring and the tall girl were engaged, if not secretly married; while certain who guessed Aunt Laura's hopes about Sabina felt sorry or amused, in accordance with their feelings to the amiable lady. And three or four men who prided themselves on knowing the world, stood in a group eyeing, when she had passed, Pen's filmy, provoking, and, on the whole, charming and desirable appearance, and decided that you had not exhausted the alternatives when you said engagement or secret marriage. You see, Pen was a stranger in Palebrook, and it is always wise to expect the worst from strangers. William was accepted into the fold on account of his relationship to the Burgers; but this girl, from Heaven knows where, with rather a foreign look, living in lodgings with her mother, who, they said, smoked and drank spirits— "Well, you know, Major, it is easy to put two and two together, though, mind you, I don't say anything. ..." Mrs. Hazard, whose life had been one of even excessive domesticity, who had been so seldom in a theatre that one of the salient events of her life which she was fain to relate was how "dear Edward," her husband, had taken her to see Henry Irving in "Becket," was coloured up by our gossips into an ex-ornament of the stage; and her cigarette-smoking, which the poor woman had begun on a physician's advice to relieve neuralgia and then kept to from habit, was taken as a minor revelation of artistic Bohemia, promising more. "Where there is smoke there is fire," as Miss Pick, who was our wit, remarked.

No sooner was the melancholy promenade over and the two returned to Mrs. Wrench's parlour, than Pen plucked off her hat and sent it spinning across the room.

"Why didn't those people stop and talk that we met? You know them all, and you went by them with your head hung down as if you were walking with a servant."

"I suppose they didn't want to stop," mumbled William. He tried to be as authoritative as he was with his mother and aunt, with Sabina too, but he was considerably cowed.

"I suppose you're ashamed of me." She was now striding to and fro in the room with an odd spasmodic lurch, twining her fingers together, and on her well-curved mouth was an ugly twist as she shot the words out. "*You* ashamed of *me!* Ha, that's good. It ought to be the other way about. I don't want to marry you. Do I, mother? You think I do? You think you can take me up and put me down when you like? I'm not good enough for your great friends? *Je suis une femme de trop, n'est-ce pas?—Ah, mais non à la fin!* It is I who do the kicking out. I simply hate you and loathe you. I've told mother a hundred times that I was sick of you."

"Then what did you want to follow me here for?" William plucked up spirits to ask.

She was momentarily staggered, less by the charge itself than by his audacity in making it. "Follow you!" her voice became almost guttural. "How dare you say that to me! It's you that ought to follow me, I should think. I suppose I can go where I like. England is a free country, isn't it? If we came here, it was just to see what kind of relations you had got. We've seen them now—the relations. Nothing doing! Why, I don't care twopence for your relations. Mother and I wouldn't be seen speaking to them again, would we, mother? They tried to cold-shoulder us at the tennis party the other afternoon to show their friends we weren't good enough. There was that Miss Molly—is that what you call her? Little insignificant creature! I've met her kind before. Lots of money, but when she opens her mouth, nobody at home. She was abominably insolent, like the rest of them."

William was stung by the injustice of this. "I'm sure they weren't. Everybody was nice to you as they could be. It's you who made all the bother, because you went about with your nose in the air as if you didn't want to be spoken to."

Pen was rather fond of giving people the lie in the intimacy of the family circle. She did it now, and slapped the table with her delicate hand. And as usual she appealed to her mother for support.

"Pen, dear, what is the good of all this excitement?" said the mother, calmly lighting a cigarette. She had weathered this kind of hurricane many times before.

So had William a few times. Although flustered, he took up his straw hat with a certain show of dignity. "I suppose you know," he ventured, "that the woman of the house and her husband can hear every word you say?"

It was a fortunate shot. Pen quieted down at once. As with many another in like case, she could control her outbursts if any inducement strong enough offered.

"It's lunch-time. I'm off," said William, looking at his watch. "My aunt told me to ask you both to her evening party on Friday, but perhaps Pen thinks we're too common to go near."

As Pen made no reply to this gamesome stroke, Mrs. Hazard, who did not much care whether she went or not, thought she was interpreting her daughter's wish, and in fact taking the wisest course, by desiring William to tell his aunt they would be glad to come.

Pen started up again. "Tell her nothing of the kind," she exclaimed. "Tell her we shall think about it."

"But I can't tell my aunt you'll think about it," remonstrated William from the doorstep.

"Then tell her nothing at all!" cried Pen, and slammed the door to underline it.

Chapter XIII

WILLIAM WALKED AWAY WITH his hands behind his back, dejected. The heteroclite character of this girl affected him like witnessing an epileptic fit. Whoever would think that she had hours of laughter and gaiety? How could he have guessed she would be like this when he proposed to her? Before that, she had for him a uniform demeanour; since, he had never seen her twice in succession in the same mood. It did not occur to him to ask whether all this might not be due to the fact that neither of them cared much for the other. Instead, his sullen musings induced him to an immense condemnation of all women. What was the good of them? They all made a puddle of men's lives.

But as a man fond of the bottle, upon waking with a headache vows he will drink no more, and then, when he sees the red wine winking in the glass and has swallowed a mouthful or two, tosses with contempt his resolution to the winds; or as one who experiences the discomforts of the rolling ship, resolves within himself nevermore to attempt the sea, but the moment past, the haven won, is ready, after a sufficient interval, to embark again—so William, upon emerging into a long road bordered with elms called The Avenue, and seeing Sabina with Ruggles slowly progressing at the far end of it, felt his indifference to womankind blown out of his head like a feather. A groom was leading away their horses, and the two, dawdling along, were chatting and laughing with a great appearance of friendliness. William regarded them in fury—the fury of a man who sees a game he has lost by his own foolishness calmly won by another. He could have stood any other man, he thought, but Ruggles. The pain in fact became intolerable, the pain of the young cock who sees the mature rooster monopolizing the attention of the hens. And as he was not much exercised in resisting his impulses, he fetched a run which soon brought him alongside of the pair.

They both looked behind them in astonishment at hearing his rapid feet; and when they saw him arrive thus panting and disordered, they wondered what calamity had befallen.

"I was only taking a little walk," explained William.

"It sounded to us like a little run," said Ruggles dryly. "Is that how you generally stroll about on a hot day? Is that how you compose your poetry?"

William looked at him and loathed him. He thought the lawyer was trying to degrade him before Sabina. And so convinced was he of the ignorance of Ruggles and of the rest of the world, except perhaps schoolmasters, on the subject of poetry, that he replied with assurance: "Never mind how I compose it. The thing is, has your memory improved?"

Ruggles wondered to see him thus brazen it out. "No," he said, "I'm afraid my memory is just where it was."

William gave an ugly laugh. "Very likely," he retorted. "We can only be young once." And with that he addressed Sabina. "We shall be late for lunch if we don't hurry. You know Uncle Herbert says he wouldn't wait for the King."

Sabina turned to Ruggles with that look of helplessness by which a woman between two men, neither of whom she wishes to offend, conveys to the one who is deserted the impression that she is being dragged off against her will.

Ruggles smiled at William. "You have all the good fortune. We saw you in the distance this morning showing Miss Hazard the sights. Ah, you poets!" And with this body-blow he turned away.

"How can you stand that fellow?" cried William, before they were out of earshot.

There was an impulsiveness, a note of warmth in this, an arrogation, as it were, of some right to control her, which sounded like the jealousy of a lover, and Sabina looked up surprised and not displeased.

"Mr. Ruggles? I think he is hugely nice. He lends me a horse and does lots of things. Don't you like him?"

"I think he's rather a rotter," said William simply.

He proceeded to explain the kind of man he did like, the picture, as it might perhaps with most of us, bearing a close resemblance to himself. How restful Sabina was after his experience that morning! How calm, well-bred, safe! No danger of a scene from her.

And Sabina listened contentedly. Seldom a woman is seriously annoyed at finding that two men are ready to cut each other's throats about her. But it might be as well to know where she was, and she flung out a sounding-line.

"I liked what I saw of Miss Hazard the other day, but she seems rather silent. Or perhaps she found me stupid. I don't understand many of her foreign allusions, though I have travelled abroad a good deal—but only with father, you know, as a tourist. Miss Hazard told me that tourists never know anything about the countries they visit. Of course, I've never studied languages and that. I'm sorry; it must be so interesting. I'm afraid I'm not clever. Now you are so clever with your poetry and so on, you must have heaps of things in common with her?"

William had formed his own opinion about Pen's mental powers, but he kept it to himself. Instead, he said what he had determined would be the safest thing to tell his aunt, that the Hazards were coming on Friday evening.

"Then I may get to know her better. I hope so. It will be so nice if they are staying at Palebrook as long as I am."

How sweet Sabina was!

"Though I know them fairly well," said William in the most careless tone he could find, "I really"—here he switched off the head of a tall weed with his stick—"know very little about their plans."

He was on the point of proposing to Sabina there and then. After all, Penelope had given him "the chuck" that very morning. But prudence reminded him that she attached very little importance to these "chucks," which were not infrequent, and unless he had it in black and white under her hand it was better to play warily.

A few hours later he had reason to congratulate himself on his restraint, when a note sent up from Palebrook was put into his hand.

> *"Mother thinks we should go to 'The Firs' on Friday*
> *evening, because she says that she is not going to have me in*
> *this shameful position any longer, and unless you tell your*
> *aunt of our engagement on Friday evening, she will."*

William set a match to this paper and held it between his thumb and finger till it burned out. What trouble a woman could bring on a man without any fault of his own! And Friday evening, instead of the exhilarating festival to which he had been looking forward not without pleasure—an evening of social intercourse unblurred by poetry— became as the date of some abominable assize.

Nor, if he had known it, was this the only terror preparing for him. Ruggles, after standing a while in the Avenue watching the other two out of sight, turned into his house and sat musing alone. The room in which he sat was precisely as it appeared in the eighteenth century—one of those white light parlours, the secret of the English eighteenth century, fragrant of lavender and rose-leaves, where the sun-light dances so gaily, and the whole aspect of the room is like a ripple of laughter—a little self-conscious, a little insincere, verily a little hard, a little cruel, but so charming! Small paintings, originals or good copies of some eighteenth-century masters—Greuze, Boucher, Fragonard— hung on the white walls; a spinet stood in one corner; porcelain bowls and jars, that happy blue and white spaced ware, rare pieces of Chelsea and Spode, were filled with flowers, a little bee droning around them;

and bright flowered poplin curtains stirred in the small wind of the summer day. Just as the room looked now must it have looked to the Mrs. Ruggles of the period, when she brought the contemporary Lady Wednesbury and a few other friends, hooped and powdered in the town fashion, back from the gazebo where they had been watching the traffic on the London road to a dish of tea or a syllabub, and a game of ombre or quadrille. And glancing out of the window at exactly the same view as the lawyer had now before his eyes, the Court ladies swung their painted fans while they discussed the virtues of tar-water, and nightgowns with mody sleeves, bone-laced caps, or sacques, and velvet patches *à la Grecque.* ...

He was not insensible to the graciousness of the room this clear day, for he was always influenced by his surroundings; and his eyes dwelt with a preoccupied complaisance upon the long stretches of lawn—among the best in the county—and the espalier roses nodding in the sunshine on the old grey wall which bordered one side of it. Only the assiduous tenderness of generations of the same family, living in peace, discharged from anxiety, could have brought this place to its ineffable perfection of detail.

But the thoughts of the owner were at present not in the house at all; they were following those other two down the Avenue. He said to himself that he was rather sick of William; he had had enough of him; it was time to put the lid on. He had always found him objectionable to connect with since his arrival at Palebrook; still, you could always minimize the connecting points, or at worst, switch off the connection altogether. But when William began to make love to Sabina Moll, to endanger the chance of the four thousand a year, he became more than a nuisance—a menace.

Then there was that Hazard girl, between whom and William he felt certain some tie existed; and with the instinct of the lawyer, always on the lookout for embarrassing and possibly criminal secrets, he would have given a good deal to learn just what the tie was. Perhaps he could get it out of the Hazard people themselves if he took an opportunity; or they might have talked to Mrs. Wrench, and Mrs. Wrench, upon whose house he had held a mortgage in a friendly way for years, would tell him anything. Meanwhile he had a bomb over there on the table which had cost him nine shillings, and he meant to explode that bomb at once. It was William's reputation as a poet which gave him his pull with Sabina; take that away and she would consider him as she did at first: an undesirable kind of animal.

Stephen's own feeling for Sabina was lukewarm: if she had not her four thousand a year it is unlikely that he would ever have thought of her at all; but girdled with that she was an acceptable, she was, in fact, the indicated wife. With four thousand a year added to his income, besides what might be expected to fall to an only daughter when her father died, he would be quite a rich man. He could allow himself the luxuries of a house in London and a yacht. And was he going to allow such an essential matter as his life to be kicked out of shape by the clumsy boot of an ass of a London clerk of no importance whatever in the world? He walked from the room with his thin face set hard—the kind of face he often wore in court when he was bringing one of his cases to a successful issue. He would blow William sky-high on Friday evening.

Chapter XIV

AND ON THAT NIGHT, accordingly, when he arrived at "The Firs," he had the bomb in the pocket of his overcoat. William, he supposed, would be asked to recite, and he would see to it that the performer was pressed to recite the "Laus Veneris." So, taking a favourable time as the evening wore on, he began mooting this here and there among the numerous company. He approached Alicia Ford, a handsome upstanding young woman with grand arms and shoulders, who besides being the champion golf and tennis player of the district, took an interest in the drama, and generally started whatever was started at the Palebrook parties.

"Hullo, Alicia! You were rather off your game yesterday at Gillingford. I lost five shillings on you. How are you going to make it up to me?"

"Any way and all ways," said Alicia in her rapid voice. "I can't afford to buy a good racket, that's what it comes to. What are we all going to get on to to-night? Gambling?"

"I've got the piece of resistance for you, Alicia—the *clou*, as your dramatic friends might call it. You have heard Mr. Spring declaim, haven't you?"

"Oh, yes, indeed!" exclaimed Alicia, who would have discussed the dark secret of her soul, if she had such a thing, at the top of her voice. "Such a nice boy he is! But his method is all wrong—no modulations. I told him so the other day. It would be simply lost in a theatre."

"He needs practice," said Ruggles. "Now, wouldn't you be doing him a good turn if you got him out to recite for us to-night?"

William heard him, white with fury and apprehension. For Penelope and her mother were present, after all.

"I could strangle that brute," thought William. "What's his game in trying to get me to recite? I'd like to spout because it makes him so jolly small, though he doesn't seem to know it. He's jealous—anybody can see that. That big Ford girl saw it. But how can I recite before Pen?"

Pen, staring straight in front of her, sat with her most forbidding air, speaking hardly at all. She was dressed in dove-grey and silver—a costume which happened to suit her perfectly, though her clothes hardly ever did. On her long fingers shone a dull bluish opal and a long emerald set in gold. The skilful eye of Aunt Laura, running over the tall thin girl, had no fault to find with her appearance, from her amber-coloured hair wreathing over the forehead like sunset clouds, to the thin, close-fitting skirt and silver-buckled shoe which cased her long, well-shaped foot with the high instep—the foot of a dancer. She only thought it a pity that Pen had not more control of her temperament, was not able to suppress her awkward moods for the benefit of other people. Still, as she agreed fully that we all live longer, or at least happier, by doing what we like, she preferred to leave Pen to get through the evening as she chose, without any futile attempts on her part to make the girl find enjoyment where she was evidently determined not to find any.

Besides, she noted with considerable annoyance that William was in marked and remarkable attendance on the Hazards, mother and daughter, though the arrangement did not seem to make for their gaiety or his own. The mother, indeed, clad in black, her spectacles dropping over her nose, her "false front" a little askew, antiquated by her daughter's will before her time, with the deprecatory look on her face of one who is habitually snubbed and suppressed, was rather ashamed of her daughter's behaviour. She herself understood that such behaviour was due more to Pen's shyness, and an excessively morbid sense of her poverty and the uncertainty of her position, than to sheer devilment and sour temper; but others could not know this, and might well object to a girl, a stranger too in Palebrook, appearing there among hospitalities, deliberately unpleasant, almost surly. Accordingly, she did her best to cover her daughter's moodiness by conciliatory words and smiles on her own part. But she was not able to make much headway under her daughter's frowns, and William was far too anxious to give her any assistance. His compromising and embarrassed conduct, in fact, made it certain for Aunt Laura that a secret tie united those three which ended her plan about Sabina. She shrugged her shoulders and went on smiling: she had done her best. It has been said that women are never philosophers; but if it be philosophy to take the rebuffs of life without agitation, then certainly she was one.

She was not alone in seeing the behaviour of William and Pen; everybody, even old Parry and the vicar, noticed it. It had a far worse effect than if they had been laughing and talking together, to see them there side by side morose. The fact is that Pen had come to the house that night determined to placard herself publicly with William, and she succeeded. Sabina noticed it; Ruggles noticed it.

If up to half-past ten Sabina had found herself for a few minutes alone with the lawyer, he would have proposed to her and she would have accepted him. But she was occupied elsewhere—at first playing and singing, and then taking a hand at cards, of which she was rather fond. Ruggles, meanwhile, considered Pen from time to time.

She did not attract him at all by her looks, his only interest in her being the interest we take in an instrument which puts the game into our hands. He had spoken to her at the tennis-party some days before, and he had not liked her. He thought her stupid and pretentious, the odious type of professional female who is always explaining or hinting that she is more important than she seems, and gives herself out as the intimate friend of the people who have employed her. Expert as he was both by nature and by his practice as a lawyer in summing up men and women, he knew exactly where Penelope fitted in the social scale, and her tall talk simply amused until it tired him. This it soon did: he found her polyglot conversation too much of a reminder of the feast of Pentecost or an international sleeping-car. He thought her too tall, too thin, and her long face quite plain; wayward, extravagant, lightly ballasted, utterly treacherous, with a disposition which in a horse would be called "vicious"—and there was the end of her so far as he was concerned.

But she might be as false and as fickle and as brain-sickly as she pleased—that was Spring's lookout, who, judging from present appearances, would have the pleasure of housing her after she was married. What concerned Ruggles and what he knew—he read it in Sabina's face over there—was that the Hazard girl had done the best part of his work for him. The finishing touch he would add in half an hour or so when the poetry began; the bomb was outside there in his overcoat pocket. On the whole, it seemed likely that those three—mother and daughter and Spring—would depart without reluctance from Palebrook by an early train and never return.

It was now half-past ten, and Penelope, who was ready to cry with boredom and temper, turned to William.

"Do you know Mr. Ruggles well?"

In William, a long evening spent in watching others following enjoyments of which he was forcibly deprived had started a condition of ferocity the worse because it must be concealed, and the name of Ruggles was like salt in a wound. He answered with great bitterness that he did not. "What's more, I don't want to."

"He is rich, isn't he?"

"Rotten," said William succinctly. "I think he's an awful-looking beast, don't you?"

Pen examined the lawyer, who was almost in a line with her at the other side of the room. "No, I don't. I think he is very distinguished. He reminds me of the Count Gomez Torrijos, whom I met at Madrid. Why can't you bring him over to talk to me?"

This was about the last thing that William desired, but he was glad of an excuse to move, and lounged off ostensibly on the errand. Pen, following him with her eyes, saw that he never went near Ruggles, and after waiting some ten minutes, she determined to act herself.

Stephen was just then standing alone in a French window which gave on the garden and was wide open to the sultry night. Pen crossed the room and made as if to pass by into the garden, but in doing so she pressed against him. A subtle heady perfume enveloped him; her hair, he thought, touched his face. She turned and said in her low, sweet voice, "I am sorry."

Was this the same creature he had been criticizing as she sat over there with William? Her face was suffused with the glamour of mystery and dream, a half-smile parted her lips tenderly, and her eyes, shy and caressing, smiled too. It was Venus, the irresistible Venus in action, who lures men whither she wills to their happiness or to their undoing. Rare enough is her apparition, for in most of those who inspire love she is not manifest; but when she does appear and puts forth her power, who can resist her?

Certainly Stephen did not. He surrendered at once. His whole being was thrilling as if he had been electrified.

"Were you going out?" he said in an unsteady voice. "I believe there are some chairs out there. Shall I find you one? Do you care to sit out a little?"

"Yes," said Pen. "Let us. The house is stifling, don't you think?"

What a voice she had, so low now that it was almost a whisper, charging her commonplace words with secret intentions, blending into harmony with the breath of the flowers on the summer night, and the soft breeze.

"Do you think I might smoke?" said Pen. "I'm simply mad for a cigarette."

Stephen produced his case and lit her cigarette, and as he did so he touched her slim fingers. She sat half-lit by the light behind, lounging back in the deep chair with her long legs crossed under her thin gown. Everything she did, her least gesture, seemed to him a marvel of grace. The very ordinary act of smoking a cigarette became invested with a strange seduction. She looked up at him standing over her and laughed a still, intimate laugh, and the light behind illumined her creamy face.

Thirty-five years with an eye kept exclusively on his own interest had tempered him; various and many had been his dealings with women, he always keeping the master-hand; but now he was swept off his feet. What had he been thinking of since Penelope Hazard had been at Palebrook? Where had his eyes been? What a stodgy fool he had been in the house there only half an hour ago!

He dropped into a chair by her and they talked. By chance Penelope had hit upon one of the men to whom her appeal was strongest—coming, and waiting for an answer—the right answer—like the cry of a dryad in a wood. She was like certain poems, or pieces of music, or pictures, which leave a few wan and troubled, while the general wonder what there is to admire. It was extraordinary how many subjects—or rather how many sensations—they had in common. How unlike she was to the mob of women one met about the county! From her residence in France and Spain she had absorbed some of the Latin captivation. Whatever she said now seemed to him miraculously right. How interesting she was about her foreign experiences; how just her comparisons were; how heartening her mirth!

"Do you sing?" he asked.

"No, alas!"

"Your speech in itself is a song."

When she rose to go in, he suggested that she should play some music, because he remembered that the piano stood apart in an alcove and he would still have her to himself. The crimson shades of the lights encrimsoned her face and hair, and she played softly, as if for him only, Schubert's Serenade, lingering on the notes with her sensuous touch. Oh, William and his poetry were well forgotten! He might claim now to be the author of *Hamlet*, if he liked.

❧

Pen's cheeks were flushed, and her eyes sparkled as she put on her cloak. Even those who disliked her appearance noticed her so far as to say that she was looking much better than usual. William tried to avoid her, but he was obliged to pass near, and he paused sheepishly.

"I'm sorry," he said, hesitating, "that I've not had a chance to speak to Aunt Laura yet. I suppose——"

"You're too stupid," she said under her breath. "Don't mention it on any account."

Just as she and her mother departed, Alicia Ford came up.

"You can't all go yet," she cried. "Mr. Spring is going to give his recitation."

"I'm going too," said Ruggles hastily. "Good night, Alicia."

So, with his two enemies off the premises, William rather willingly attacked "Laus Veneris" again.

Chapter XV

MRS. HAZARD TURNED UP THE lamp and sank into a chair in Mrs. Wrench's parlour.

"Oh, I'm glad this evening is over. I'm so tired!" She thought it good tactics to be first in the field with her complaints.

Pen hummed as she squirted the siphon-water into the glass.

"Didn't you like it? I thought it was awfully nice. I enjoyed myself thoroughly." She sipped her drink, lighted a cigarette, and pulling her gown up over her knees, sat down. "I feel awfully well, mother. I'd like to go out and walk for miles and miles. You see, I'm happy, and I always feel well when I'm happy."

"That's right, dear," said the mother, surprised and relieved. "I told you that you might like it if you went. I'm sure I enjoyed my game of bezique with that Miss Ford myself. It was nice of her to propose it, seeing me sitting alone. Isn't that the girl Mrs. Wrench told us of whom the man who is always playing billiards at the hotel and betting on races is in love with? I can't think of his name. He wasn't there, was he? Mrs. Wrench says they don't invite him. Oh, Pen, you never ordered the cigarettes to-day, and there are only two more in the tin."

Pen was lost in thought. She stood up and looked at herself in the distorting mirror over the fire-place. "I rather like myself in this dress. It's better style altogether than the mixy-mauvey things most of those other girls had on. Mr. Ruggles thinks I'm handsome—at least, he didn't say it in so many words, but he did indirectly. Now I shouldn't call myself handsome, would you?"

"My dear, I think you're very attractive," said the mother, trying to keep her interest alive enough to say the right thing.

"I'll tell you what a person—well, a man—I've told you about him before—said to me once. He said, 'You're not handsome, you're worse.'" Pen clapped her hands on her hips, flung back her head, and laughed at herself in the mirror. "Ruggles found that to-night. He was jolly well captured." She laughed again with pleasure. "I think he's rather nice-looking, don't you?"

The mother was baffled. "I'm not sure that I know who he is, Pen. Which was Ruggles? There were so many of them."

"The man with the clean-shaven face and black hair. Do you mean to say you didn't see us together? William did; he was wild with jealousy. It was too killing. William was awfully dull. He's such a boy. I don't care about boys."

She went to bed in high spirits; but her night must have been troubled, for in the morning she had breakfast in bed, and it was between eleven and twelve before she appeared downstairs, clad in a dressing-gown and looking white and listless.

"I have a frightful headache. I couldn't eat any breakfast."

"Poor Pen!" sympathized the mother, who had heard the reverse from Mrs. Wrench.

"I've been thinking over the conduct of that man last night. It was rather insulting. I let him go too far, don't you think?"

"Oh no, my dear, I shouldn't think so," said the mother, who had not the faintest notion what man it was or how far he had gone.

"He tried to squeeze my hand—at least he touched it two or three times, and I know it wasn't by accident. He did it on purpose. He must think I'm pretty free-and-easy if I overlook that in a man I've only met twice. Then his looks were—well, suggestive."

"Were they?" Mrs. Hazard murmured pacifically. "He probably didn't mean anything."

"Didn't mean anything!" Pen began to pace up and down and the mother saw the storm was inevitable. She only hoped it would be short. "Didn't mean anything! Really, mother, I can't make you out. You don't seem to care twopence what becomes of your children. It is all one to you whether your daughter is grossly insulted or not. Do you mean to say you are willing to sit there and let that man Ruggles think he can take any liberties with me he chooses? You say he didn't mean anything! I know what he meant: I'm not a child. Would you like to have a daughter who let any man who comes along make love to her? I say his behaviour was insulting, and if you won't take it up I shall simply write to Jack or Cyril about it. As it is, I shall tell William the moment he comes."

"Pen, dear! How can you be so silly?" exclaimed the mother, roused at length. If her daughter did bring down her sons, on whose common sense she had no reliance whatever, she would assuredly be placed in a disagreeable and ridiculous position. "You can't want a scandal in this place about nothing, can you? What did the man do to you to cause all this fuss?"

"I know what he did. I saw it. It is so horribly unfair to William, too, who is breaking his heart about me."

"But did you tell him you were engaged to William?"

"How could I tell him, after promising William not to? I wonder you don't take a little more interest."

"Oh, Pen, I really won't stand these continual scenes any longer!" cried the mother. "I wish you'd get married and have done with it. If you take my advice, you won't have a scandal. My opinion is—I know you think nothing of it, but I've lived longer than you have, and my opinion is that a woman, and especially an unmarried girl, should overlook anything and everything rather than have a scandal. What do you want me to do now? Do you want me to go to Mr. Ruggles, and tell him you're engaged to William, and ask him to explain his conduct?"

But Pen was not prepared for direct action of this kind. "It wouldn't do much good if you did. I know that kind of man. He's not the honest John Bull like William. He'd tell a lie to your face as soon as look at you. He'd say he didn't know what you were talking about. And as there's no proof——"

At this point a box and a great bunch of flowers were brought in. They had been left by Mr. Ruggles' servant with his master's compliments.

Pen frowned at the offerings. "I vote we send them back," she said, after waiting till the maid had left the room. "I hate his attentions."

"I don't think I should do anything quite so marked," replied Mrs. Hazard, humouring her.

"At any rate, we shan't open the cigarette-box till I've spoken to William," decided the daughter. "As for the flowers, you can do what you like with them. They haven't cost him much. He has miles of glass-houses."

And when William turned up a little later, the first thing she did was to tell him that Mr. Ruggles had sent her a huge box of cigarettes.

William stared, utterly puzzled. "Ruggles? To your mother, you mean," he brought out at length.

"No, I mean to me." She tapped with her foot impatiently. Now that William was there before her eyes, her emotions turned chill. No, there was no doubt about it: as a lover William was decidedly inferior to the other.

But William's amazement grew. "What on earth should Ruggles want to send cigarettes to you for?" he blurted.

It must be explained that he saw hardly any physical charm in Pen. He had indeed become engaged to her, and he could never give a very lucid account to himself of that event. Her generosity in lending money might have had something to do with it, but certainly it had not happened because he thought her handsome, or even pretty. He had never heard those of his friends upon whose judgment he was disposed to rely in these subjects approve of anything about her except her height, and even then they hedged by saying she was too thin. Therefore, that the lawyer would send things to Pen out of disinterested admiration was the very last explanation to occur to him; and as his speculations never moved very far from the centre, he could see in the action nothing else but an ironical cut at him and his flirtation with Sabina. He hated the lawyer more than ever, but he could not very well give his real reason to Penelope; and as he had not the least glimmering of jealousy where she was concerned, he did not think of bringing that into play as a motive.

"Very generous of the old buck," he sneered; but Pen's ear was not to be misled in such matters, and she perceived that whatever else the sneer implied, it did not imply jealousy.

She fingered the box. "Then you think it's all right?" she asked detachedly, to satisfy her scruples.

"What's all right?"

"Mother seemed to think I ought to send them back."

William gave a loud guffaw. "Send back five hundred expensive cigarettes! She must be crazy. What on earth for?"

Pen sliced open the box, took a cigarette, and shoved the box over to William.

"Will you have one?"

"Rather," said William.

Chapter XVI

HE LUNCHED ALONE WITH his aunt, and as they lingered over the end of the meal, she said casually: "William, dear, you might go sailing with your uncle and Sabina this afternoon."

"I thought she was riding."

"Yes, but Stephen has sent up a note to say that the horse she rides has gone lame. It's rather tiresome: I'm so sorry for Sabina. So your uncle is going to take her on the water, and I fancied that you might go too. But I suppose you are engaged with the Hazards."

She spoke as one who shouts victory in the shadow of defeat. She had now only a fragment of hope that the affair of her nephew and Sabina would unravel as she wished. Still, it is well to act as if what you desire is certain.

"No," said William, "I've nothing to do." He added after due reflection, for he was a young man of extreme caution in his utterances: "By the way, Ruggles has taken them up for all he's worth."

"The Hazards?"

William nodded. "He sent them a lot of flowers and cigarettes this morning."

This did give her a shock: it was about the last thing she expected to hear. That Stephen, of all men, should go out of his way to pay marked attention to people like the Hazards, who had no importance and scarcely a foothold anywhere, was what she could hardly believe. She cast about for motives, but could find none beyond the daughter's attractiveness—seeing that, indeed, much plainer than William, but still with an eye altogether unenthralled, which estimated the attractiveness as being on the whole moderate.

"You know all about the Hazards, don't you?"

"Yes," replied William. "All there is to be known."

"They have no well-known relations, or anything like that?"

William made the mistake of thinking that this remark was levelled at himself. "Oh, I don't know so much about that," he grumbled. "Their grandfather or something was a Lord Mayor."

Aunt Laura smiled pensively with her forefinger pressed on her cheek. She did not think this ancestral Mayor would cut much of a figure with the lawyer. No, it must be the girl; and if so, all sorts of possibilities opened up. Sabina, for one thing, would be rather neglected, and the lame nag struck her for the first time in the shape of a lame excuse.

"Be sure you're awfully nice to Sabina!" she cried with heightened courage.

"Aren't you coming?"

"Oh, no. I never go out of my depth. You don't want me to do *all* your lovemaking for you, do you?"

"No," replied William thoughtfully, "I don't think I do—not now. But I like you to be about. When you're there I get along better;" a remark which showed that at last he understood he must play warily and needed skill.

"Oh, you will get along all right. Just plunge in and trust to luck." She spoke gaily.

The day was not altogether lost; the ground had shifted to her advantage. If Stephen was really serious about Penelope, which seemed too good and too untoward to be true, Aunt Laura did not think that in view of the large opulent life opened out before her, the Hazard girl was the kind of girl to let any affection she might feel for a mere clerk at Ibed's stand in her way.

And Sabina, resenting his desertion, would concentrate her wavering sympathies on William. Luckily, Sabina was no longer a young girl; she must be well over twenty-five; and Aunt Laura thought she knew that women when they reach that age make a great case of youth in men. She reflected with complacency that Ruggles as a rival to William would be much more dangerous with a younger girl than with Sabina. Ruggles, she thought, cold and self-contained as he was, had some touch in him of the romantic lover, of the man who would venture desperate issues for love if once he were deeply engaged, and William certainly had not; but then, on a final analysis, neither Ruggles nor William, unless her tests were all wrong, was in love with Sabina. In a word, after unprejudiced study of the weights, age, and state of the course, it seemed pretty safe to bet that, if the weather held good, William would arrive in first.

Chapter XVII

PENELOPE CAME DOWN FROM her bedroom to the parlour about four o'clock. She had not been out of doors all day. The parlour was empty: her mother was at the back of the house gossiping with Mrs. Wrench. Pen wore a gown of myrtle green *crêpe de Chine* pulled up by the long loop of her girdle. It left her neck bare, and the long light sleeves called attention to her lithe hands. She took up a magazine, sat down by the half-open window and crossed her legs, and her patent-leather shoes with silver buckles emphasized her poppy-coloured openwork stockings.

A gentle sun penetrated through the room, and on the chimney-piece the bunch of fresh-gathered flowers which had come that morning glowed. From time to time Pen shoved back the curtain a little and threw a look into the street as if she were expecting some one; then she glanced at the clock, a smile glided over her lips, and nonchalantly, with her long frail hand on which there were three rings she arranged the loose hair on her forehead.

"Will he come?" she thought. She remembered his words, still more his looks of the night before, and she thought it likely he would. He had sent the flowers and cigarettes with sufficient promptitude. The

flowers added an unexpected touch, like a caress, which indicated certainly that he had her saliently in his mind. The impression she had
made, then, had out-lasted the night; would it be still strong enough to
send him here this afternoon? She herself had developed, on top of her
resentment of this morning, a strong desire to see him again, which
arose partly, no doubt, from the vanity of having a man in her power
and the wish to gratify it still more by seeing him there in front of her
to play upon, but also because she was really attracted to him by the
profound differences as well as by certain astonishing coincidences of
their characters.

In fact, if Stephen were anxious to be received well by her, he could
not find a better moment to walk in. The inevitable reaction from her
scruples of the morning was in full force. William's indifference, she
considered, was enough to exonerate her if she went to any lengths she
pleased; and into the bargain she was rather piqued by his obvious lack
of jealousy.

"What a fool I am," she thought, "to mind about William or any one
else in these matters. I'd make love to the devil if I felt like it," she added
wantonly, stretching out her arms.

In fact, from the moment William went out of the house, till now,
she had given herself full rein to consider Stephen as a possible lover, and to debate what form her response would take. At present she
was decided that she would respond if he gave her the least invitation.
Although with Pen revulsion generally was at the heels of desire, still
her desires had an immense vitality in their changeableness; for the
imaginative conception of another pleasure more attractive, more
perfect, reanimated them suddenly. Then were they born again, rapid
as the thunder, irresistible, ardent, more vast, stretching from point
to point till the very frame of possibility was broken. They had the
charm of sweetening, for some few hours at all events, the bitterness of
a thousand shocks to her self-esteem. They ran towards the unknown,
towards the impossible, braving satiety in the continual search for a
new sensation, for the pleasure which would be supreme and ideal.
Then suddenly they collapsed, smashed by their very violence, worn
out by the sterility of their efforts. ...

However, at this moment she was at the top of the wave. She continued to contemplate for nearly an hour, in a solitude which nobody
came to break, the new horizon which had suddenly appeared to her.

Indeed, she had worked herself into such a state of confidence that the sound of feet in the passage made her start, and when the door-handle rattled, a fugitive colour crept into her cheeks. But it was her mother who entered.

"Ah!" cried Pen, horribly disappointed. "It's you!"

"Yes, it's me." She sat down and lit a cigarette. "How good these cigarettes are that man sent. I'm smoking them all." She examined her daughter inattentively. "You've changed your frock, haven't you? Are you expecting any one?"

This question irritated Pen.

"Good heavens, mother, you seem always in a dream lately! I believe you smoke too much. Who is there for me to expect in this rotten little town? You know they don't call on us—or at least they haven't up to now, except William's aunt, who condescended so far. I changed my dress because I had nothing else to do. I'm bored to death."

She said all that with her most exasperating smile, and in a tone of raillery which presaged nothing good.

"I thought," said Mrs. Hazard, taking it lightly, "that you said you had a number of things to do this afternoon."

"Yes, so I had. But when I have a lot of things to do, I never want to do one of them."

The mother, finding nothing politic to answer, just blew out a puff of smoke. Pen glanced again at the clock; it was too late for him to come now. She listened, but hearing no sound in the house she rose abruptly.

"Blow it all!" she cried passionately.

She banged down the window to close out the noises of the street, and flung herself at full length upon an old horse-hair sofa in the last quarter of its life, drawn up near the fire-place in which a small fire agonized. She lay flat on her back staring at the ceiling, the poor, wasted, poppy-coloured stockings showing in all their garishness, with such an expression of dumb revolt on her face that her mother dared not speak. Nothing at all had happened; things were where they had been all day; and yet it seemed to Pen as if she had just been the victim of some definite calamity which had made a ruin of her life. And she pondered desperately on her present state, and the future which awaited her. A field spread before her vast and dreary. It was the field of regrets, of vain aspirations, of insatiable desires which could never be realized.

A sense of tedium without limits overwhelmed the girl. In her mind, in her heart, she could find only emptiness, an immense vacuity, the aridity of an infinite Sahara.

"What have I ever had to enjoy since I was born? My childhood went by without any pleasure, and I had all the miseries and mortifications of a poor girl at a boarding-school who has to refuse to join in the plans of the others because her people don't send her any money. As for love, all my flirts have turned out badly either through my own silliness, or through the kind of men I took up with. All those brutes of men who took me out to dinner, and wanted to kiss me in the taxi, and were always asking me to keep it quiet. Never again will I have anything to do with a man who wants to keep it quiet, either because he is married, or something else. The fathers of families who take so much interest in their daughters' lessons—they're the most anxious of all to keep it quiet. If I didn't feel so furious just now I could laugh at the thought of them—the way they breathe down my neck and keep feeling for my fingers. Now I'm engaged to William, and he's like the others,—though he doesn't feel much for my fingers or anything else. But he wants to keep it quiet too, damn him! He's no help; a life with him isn't exactly gay to look forward to. I may even have to take pupils to help out expenses. I've only met one man I really loved and whom I could have lived with happily, poor or rich; and I fought with him. As for the rest, they're all about the same price. All? ... Well, perhaps——"

She pulled up one of the cushions which were on the sofa, turned on her side with her back to her mother, and covered her face with her hands the better to concentrate her thought.

"There is this Mr. Ruggles. I'm not in love with him—not in the least—but I think I could like him awfully. He looks a bit hard, but what a lot of will there is in his face! If that man fell in love—really in love—he oughtn't to be like the others. I'm certain he hasn't the every-day young-man-at-the-tennis-party sentiments and silly conceit and self-importance of William Spring. He looks as if he was able to get what he wants done, instead of talking about the fine things he can do. And if he married, he would know how to be master of his wife, and in case of a struggle to break her and bring her to his feet, without her ceasing to love him a single minute."

At this thought Pen flung herself round on the couch with a look of admiration in her feverish eyes, swimming in the vast sea of her fantasy with no other pilot than her caprice, and fearing only to touch land. ...

Her mother, plunged in an absorbing page of *What Every Woman Ought to Know*, thought she was asleep, but chancing to look up, and seeing her daughter lying there with eyes staring into vacancy, she took this very inopportune moment to remark:

"Perhaps William will look in by and by."

Pen came to herself with a jerk.

"William," she repeated.

She considered her mother with an indefinable look: her eyes had that composite expression which must be called sphinx-like, but the dominating sentiment was a rather contemptuous pity.

"Whatever makes you want to force William on me? It's not as if he was a great catch. He's no catch at all. Did you ever realize what my life with William will be? It will be the same as home, only worse. And I detest it, I'm sick of it, and loathe it."

She was whipping herself into a state of violent excitement. Her complexion of an olive pallor became suddenly coloured, the glitter in her eyes was like fever, the blood pounded in her veins, and she struck the sofa with her open hand.

"You must remember," said the mother, coolly wiping her spectacles, "that he was your own choice. He comes of nice people and you might do worse. But I accept him because he's there. When I told you we ought to see his mother at the house, you shut me up. I had nothing to do with it. You and the boys arranged it between you."

"Yes," agreed Pen, "that's all right. And I suppose I'll marry him. I may and I may not. I suppose it's more of an advantage in some ways for a woman to be married than single. But if you think that I'm looking forward to marrying a junior clerk in Ibed's! Why, it will be everything I hate. The wretched smelly little flat; William going every morning to the office, and coming home every evening from the office. And I'll have to sit facing him every night in the little room with the stained tablecloth after the supper is cleared away; and we'll treat ourselves to the half-crown seats at the theatre every three months; and we'll have no money for jewellery and frocks and hats—no money for anything outside the house. That's what marrying William means, and I abominate all that. I detest the *tous les jours*. Do you see me the wife of a little clerk? And to be patronized by Aunt Laura, who thinks she does us so much honour by asking us to her house because she's rich and we're not any more, and who will send her nephew's wife presents of her old frocks, and a turkey at Christmas!—Oh, no—not that part of it for me!—Never!"

She ended almost on a shout, her melodious voice piteously jangled, her face sombre, her mouth bitter and awry, her fingers twitching.

"I feel stifling," she said, putting her hand on her side. "My head is on fire. I've got neuralgia all over and I don't care twopence."

There was a pause, and Mrs. Hazard said:

"Do you think we used as much sugar as that this week?" She was examining the grocer's bill.

"I did happen to see his mother, if you want to know," Pen went on more quietly. "He took me to lunch with her one day at the Great Central Hotel. She looks almost as young as I do; she's awfully smart and well-dressed. She couldn't be serious, a woman like that; she was flippant the whole time. I did ask her to come out and see you, and she said her morals weren't good enough. What do you think of that for a mother?"

She jumped from the sofa and threw open the window to breathe some air and try to recover a little calm. Just at that moment a man on horseback was passing at foot-pace before the house.

"Mr. Ruggles!" she murmured.

She flung at him such a look of fever and invitation and perversity that a magnetic current was established between them, and during a few seconds they remained as if fascinated by one another. He pulled up his horse.

"Wait a minute. I'll come in if I may," he said.

There was an inn a few yards below on the opposite side of the street. She saw him dismount and hand over his horse to the yardman.

"Mr. Ruggles is coming, mother," cried Pen.

"Oh, is he?" said Mrs. Hazard, straightening her "false front." Her daughter had suddenly become radiant, so she judged that the visitor was to be welcomed. From where she sat she had intercepted the incandescent look—eyes and eyebrows and lips all together in it—which Pen had given the lawyer, and recalling the tirades of this morning, she thought that if Pen had used that sort of lure the night before, no man could be blamed for any liberties he took. But she was a woman not without sense, and having found that her daughter's temperament was there for good, she had long ago ceased to interfere even with its most disconcerting manifestations.

Chapter XVIII

IT WAS THE LOOK from the window that did the business for Stephen. He had admired Penelope the evening before, he had even been profoundly stirred by her; but he was very far from considering her in any light which could affect his designs. He thought he knew her character, and it was one of those characters which the wise man who seeks not occasions of annoyance, or perhaps disaster, deals with sparingly. He felt he would be glad to see her again should an unforced opportunity occur; but if not—well, not. His resolution to marry Sabina was not in the least altered; the lame horse, so far from being an excuse, as Aunt Laura imagined, was standing there with his leg bandaged in the stable; and indeed at the very moment he rode down the street, he was thinking that he had been a fool to give William a second life. Then he met her look, and William and Sabina and everybody else became to him as unimportant as clouds drifting across the stars.

As he crossed the street he hit upon an excuse to cover his appearance, and this, once in the room, he brought out to Mrs. Hazard, offering her the use of one of his motors in case she felt disposed to explore the neighbourhood.

"You have only to send up Mrs. Wrench's boy with a message whenever you want it. My driver knows the country like the palm of his hand."

Mrs. Hazard said her thanks, and if she had not been so used to take most things as a matter of course, she might have been surprised at this offer from a man she hardly knew. But in Pen it reached its right address, and when she gave him a quick, tender glance of gratitude, he blessed himself for his lucky thought.

He had come into the full benefit of the reaction. Very animated, Pen was using all the resources of her temperament, and revealed a subtle kind of witchery that her mother, who had always seen her disdainful or moody with the men who came to their house, never dreamed she had at command. And she thought it must have been with her present manner that her daughter had attracted all those foreign men she was for ever talking about, whose infatuation Mrs. Hazard had hitherto found it difficult to understand.

The fact is that Stephen's offer, which to some will appear paltry enough, was just the kind of thing to make Pen reverberate. It seemed to her large, considerate, generous, the act of a man indifferent to what other people said, and above the smallnesses of life. She liked to meet with a man who could walk in and hand over a motor-car and driver in a breath; it was a pleasant change from those eternal men in London who thought they were cutting quite a figure if they took you in a taxi-cab. Her ruling snobbery—her only one really—was the snobbery of position; and this is easily understood if you consider that she had generally found herself situated in direct inferiority to other people, whether to her pupils and their parents as governess, or as here now at Palebrook, where for all her boasting and scoffing, for all the ancestral Lord Mayor, she felt in her heart of hearts that she was an outsider, a waif, almost an adventuress (this word used to send a shudder down her spine), as contrasted with the rigid line of the well-to-do families in the place. She saw the insignificance of this "rigid line" in relation to the world at large as clearly as you could; but to revert to Pascal's maxim, she had now been long enough in Palebrook to mind the opinion of the inhabitants. Besides, "the world at large"—what, after all, was that? Little, smug, self-satisfied Palebrook was the world and the world's opinion to those who lived in it, and she was in a mood to accept the absurd little place on its own terms.

And of all these people in Palebrook, here, sitting in front of her, was the unquestioned chief. Whoever else rode loosely at their anchors, he was infallibly harboured. He was one who had all the guarantees, who might pass confident, as much as anyone could, in the obscure chaos of hours to be lived, of which we know no more the number than we can count the smiles and the tears.

So, looking at him through half-closed eyes, Pen laughed her low, gurgling laugh, with all the melody of her voice and all the whiteness of her teeth. To Stephen she seemed adorable thus, with her head thrown back, her firmly moulded throat quivering in this joyous outburst which shook her long frame, and her hair rather disordered from lying on the sofa—a Bacchante, he thought, in a hired parlour; where indeed your Bacchantes are not seldom to be found awaiting the passage of the golden chariot with the joy-giving god.

He forgot the time, and might have sat on for hours if Mrs. Wrench's little maid had not come bustling in with the tablecloth. Pen gave her a petrifying look, but the spell was broken, and Stephen remembered he was to dine at Palebrook Court. In the passage, Mrs. Wrench herself stood timidly to pay her respects to the great man.

"Good evening, Mrs. Wrench," he said. "I hope you are making these ladies comfortable."

It was as good as a command, and Pen, delighted, saw from the look on Mrs. Wrench's face that her opinion of her lodgers had gone up with a bound. If the great Mr. Ruggles came and sat with them for nearly an hour, and took an interest in their well-being, they must be more important people than the landlady had fancied. "There's a man!" thought Pen, and she watched his back down the street with admiring eyes. He had done by chance the one thing he could have done to please her most. The landlady's sudden obsequiousness was balm of Gilead upon all the tiny wounds to her self-esteem she had suffered since she came to Palebrook. She thought of the ineffectual William, and of his aunt, who was apparently so anxious to make it clear that they were just acquaintances, and she almost loved Ruggles.

"Don't you like him, mother?" she asked, coming back into the room.

"Gertie has just been telling me that he's the great man here." Mrs. Hazard was lighting a cigarette. "He seems very nice. Very quiet and easy and all that."

"He's a darling!" cried Pen enthusiastically. She leant out of the window to get another glimpse of him, and was just in time to see him run into a railway porter, who was perhaps dreaming of collisions. Pen felt quite indignant with the porter.

"Why couldn't the stupid lout get out of the way?—But if he"—this was not the porter—"walks without taking notice he must be thinking, and I'll bet he's thinking of me."

Then, later, when the implements of supper were gone, "Mother," said Pen, "I am going to cut the cards and see what my fortune says."

"A dark man is thinking of me," quoth she, after a moment.

"I thought as much," said the mother to herself.

❧

Oh yes, her dark man was thinking of her right enough. He thought of her through Lady Wednesbury's disquisitions on music—she played the violin—and through her husband's criticism of the Government's action in Ireland, where he spent part of every year.

"They ought to settle it," he said. "They have their hands free of foreign complications—at least, I suppose so. There's that row in the Balkans—do you suppose they mean to land us into that?"

"Who can tell?" said Stephen absentmindedly, his thoughts in Mrs. Wrench's parlour.

Afterwards, as he strolled homeward through the park in the summer moonlight, he was thinking of her still. But his thoughts ran in cross-currents; they made by no means the steady stream of tendency in her direction which Pen saw as she lay on her back in bed down there at Palebrook, dreaming ... dreaming. ...

"If I don't look out," he was saying to himself, "I shall be utterly in love with that girl. I'm three-quarters in love with her already. I wonder does she care for me? Her looks say a good deal, but she has evidently seen a lot of a kind of life which our girls here in Palebrook never see. Who was it was telling me she took drugs?—I forget; I was not interested in her then and I paid no attention. The question is, am I going to throw away four thousand a year and more for five feet ten of nerves and hysteria?"

He pictured to himself with extreme lucidity life in common with Penelope: her moods, her whims, which he had seen; her sulks and scruples, which he suspected. But such as she was, he wanted her at this instant more than he wanted anything—the tall, phantasmic tower of ivory. He saw her as intensely as if she were there on the road before him, smiling that ambiguous smile of hers, with the eyes half-closed, the head thrown back, the tongue just showing between the little teeth. No girl in Palebrook could smile like that. It was the result of a special education, the most complex influences, a sounding of the most emotional mysticism and (he felt almost inclined to say) the most audacious depravity. A smile from her meant less than a smile, say, from Jessie Bartlet or the other Palebrook prettinesses; but it also meant more. ...

"I wonder just where she is with that man Spring? I know where he is with her—that is, where he is now, not where he has been."

He looked hard at this, and beneath his scrutiny one aspect of the affair emerged. Stephen had more than once thought himself in love, but comparing what he could remember of his past sensations with what he felt for Pen, they seemed like the flicker of a few matches to a burning city. And yet in this case, no more than in some others, were love and the purpose of marriage paragenic: with a man of his experience, used by profession to having the seamy side of things presented to him, it would have been strange if they were. He was not more strait-hearted and selfish than most of his fellows, and a good deal less than some; but he was what is called a man of the world, and your man of the world is given to look for shabby motives in actions apparently generous, and to distrust the first movements of his heart.

What he saw was a girl who did not look a neophyte, who looked in fact as if she had already shared a variegated experience and was prepared for more, dropping out of a cloudy past on Palebrook, accompanied by a person who might be her mother, and again who might not, for they bore no resemblance to each other. And this girl arrived shortly after a young man to whom she was tied in some way which could not be publicly avowed, and whom she treated, and by whom she was treated, in a manner which betokened a passion at its lees rather than love honestly come by and rejoicing. Her gestures, things she let slip, a thousand trifles which others—Aunt Laura, for instance—let pass unheeded, but which the trained observation of the lawyer carefully noted, betrayed one who had not lived—say, like Sabina, secluded and barricaded; but one who had thrown herself into life as a graceful swimmer in to a river, who had been free with the world, and with whom possibly the world had been free. Sabina looked single, almost a spinster, to the most unpractised eye; a shop-boy would call her "miss"; but Pen was one of those girls who set strangers betting whether they are single or married, with odds on married. Stephen liked her the better for all this; in fact, the type of Sabina did not appeal to him at all and the type of Pen most powerfully did. In his eyes, Sabina was just a nice little girl; and Pen was the siren, the goddess, what you like, who captures mortals by the magic of her eyes and voice and the knots of her hair. But then in the world's eyes Pen was at best a nobody, and at worst, as it might turn out, too well known a body; while Sabina, flanked by great interests, had four thousand a year. He loved Pen—there was no doubt about that; but from manifold reasons, social and personal, he was not prepared to marry her. And he asked himself if he could not gain his ends without marriage.

He was now come to his own gate, and he leant on the bars looking at the sweet old house basking in the moonlight among the flowers. In the thin haze which overhung the sward, phantoms of his ancestors, whose hand had been felt so long on Palebrook, moved fantastically, white-faced and dishevelled. And he asked himself if he could not gain his ends without marriage. Possibly he could. With Spring, whatever he counted for, got out of the way by being given a clear run with Sabina, Pen, seeing her character, would probably veer definitely round to him if he showed himself assiduous and generous.

But even as he figured this, he saw it was not what he wanted. If he did take a step which made his relations closer with Pen, he could never bear life apart from her. His jealousy of Spring might warn him of the unsupportable obsessions which would in that case ensue. Pen living apart from her lover would make the ambiguity of her position an excuse to take all the liberties, and that would mean atrocious suffering and a break. Even if it did not come quite to that—think of the continual scenes, accusations, regrets! No, if he had her at all, it must be to sit with him in yonder house, to go about with him publicly. It must be marriage or nothing. So the matter narrowed down to this: Was he enough in love with Pen to marry her, and shoulder the various consequences, some of them disagreeable enough, of such an act?

He came to the conclusion, as he walked up the drive, that he was not.

Chapter XIX

WITH THE INEVITABLENESS OF everything else in Palebrook, where life followed the hour with an unvarying result, Ruggles used to motor over every Tuesday and Friday to Gillingford, where he had another office. Pen's mind had been full of him since his visit, and as was always the case with her, she felt an imperious need to talk about what was in her mind. She talked about him to her mother till the mother ceased even to pretend an interest, and then she fell back on Mrs. Wrench, who admired and respected the lawyer more than any man on earth. Mrs. Wrench gave her the information about Gillingford.

For the last four days Pen had been in a turmoil, restless, feverish, eating badly, and, in spite of her drugs, lying awake long hours at night. She even gave up her drugs one night, preferring, she said, to lie awake so that she could think. And the burthen of her thoughts was: Is he in love with me?

She had not much to go on; since his visit she had not seen him again; but all the same, she thought he was. Her instinct, as she put it, told her he was. Love, where both parties are interested, can get on with wonderfully little signalling. Suppose he were to marry her: what a change in her life! And her eyes wide open in the twilight of the flickering night-light, her pulses beating, she dreamed of this triumphant refutation of her past. No more cruel lessons to unruly or stupid children, no more insolence from parents, no more journeys by omnibus, and bedraggled skirts on wet days. Instead, she would be the first woman in Palebrook, and a good second anywhere else. Oh, Heaven, what an outcome! And, as ever in her visions, she looked beyond the mark, neglecting such realities as came between.

When at length she recalled her engagement to William, she dropped down out of the blue like a spent lark. Did she love William? It didn't matter; she had to be loyal to him—at least she supposed so. For the matter of that, did she love the other man?

"Do you think I'm in love with him, mother?"

"No, my dear, I shouldn't think so." The answer was perfunctory. "You can't very well be, can you?"

"I don't know so much about that. He's just the kind of man I always wanted, even when I was a kid. Oh, I know what you think. You think it wouldn't be fair to William. But I don't see why I should always consider William. I'll marry him, I suppose, as I promised to, but I can't help my thoughts, can I?"

"No, of course not," murmured Mrs. Hazard, who was reading a chapter on the treatment of crying babies in *What Every Woman Ought to Know*, which absorbed her far more than her daughter's love affairs. It would be time enough to think about them when they did begin to look like marriage.

❧

But if Pen considered herself bound to be loyal to William, she was not in the least disposed to let him overlook the sacrifice. Whenever the young man presented himself she was either snappish or contemptuous. She was always mentally comparing him to Stephen, and to his disadvantage. She was bound to him, she knew that, and she meant to stick to him, but there was surely no harm in being alive to his faults.

She herself hardly mentioned Ruggles; but for William the lawyer had the same fascination as whatever we abhor or fear has for most of us. When, standing with his back to the empty fire-place in his favourite attitude, hands deep in trouser pockets and long legs wide apart, William started to exercise his wit on Ruggles, Pen took the offensive. Somebody—an actor she knew—had told her Swift's saying, that nobody but a fool ever wished he were younger; the phrase had struck her and she had treasured it for future use. She used it now.

"Oh, that's all right," laughed William in his easiest style. "Some old blokes have seen a bit of life, I expect. I should prefer my uncle, myself."

"You know, William," said Pen, speaking in the candid tone of one who is obliged against her will to state an unpleasant fact—the best tone she could have pitched upon to annoy him, "you will be a horrible man when you are thirty. I can picture you now."

Mrs. Hazard managed to smooth him down, and he made some excuse and hurried away.

For the rest, he paid little attention just at this time to the things Pen said, and abbreviated the opportunities for saying them. No doubt he would marry her ultimately; he had to be loyal to her—at least he supposed so. Meanwhile, he was employed elsewhere. In those days he was, so to speak, laying up treasure in Manchester. Sabina was on his hands; for Ruggles, who had hitherto shared with him that weight, seemed to be during the last week so multifariously engaged that he was regarded from "The Firs" as having tired of the tourney and abandoned the field. This at least was the opinion of Mr. Burger—no mean judge in such matters, so the Palebrook Club thought. In that establishment they were punting heavily on the result, and showed an indecent anxiety for "tips."

Sabina did not seem to mind about Stephen's remissness, and when Pen saw her on Tuesday with a numerous party, William among them, going down to the quay, evidently on a boating expedition, she appeared in what might pass, in so very minor-keyed a little person, for high spirits.

The sight of Sabina counted no more for Pen than that of any other passer in the street; but William's presence in the company was not without influence on her actions. She came down at about half-past two this same Tuesday afternoon dressed for walking. Mrs. Hazard rose to get ready.

"You needn't come unless you like mother. I'd much prefer to be alone."

Her mother looked at her with astonishment, for since they had been in Palebrook the daughter had refused to stir a step out of doors without the mother tagged to her side. And when she heard that Pen might be absent as long as two hours she was also relieved; it was so much time gained for her book, her cigarettes, possibly sleep, certainly peace.

Penelope had decided to walk out of Palebrook on the Gillingford road. It was Tuesday: she might meet him returning. Of course there was a very good chance she might not; be might stay late, or he might be returned earlier; and she served herself with this uncertainty to silence her scruples. Then the thought of William with the boating-party definitely strangled them.

"He goes about enjoying himself without thinking of me. I don't see why I should always consider him. He's frightfully selfish."

She walked on faster with her loping, graceful walk. In a mirror which stood in a shop-window she caught sight of herself and she thought she looked handsome, in spite of the nervous fatigue in which she had lived during the last few days. A few people turned to look at her, but it was the strangeness, the foreignness of her appearance which took their eye rather than her beauty, which, as has been said, was not of a kind to appeal to the majority; and this was made plain by the fact that as many women looked after her as men.

The Gillingford road was straight and dusty and full of traffic. Motors and char-à-bancs, traps and bicycles, coming most of them from a well-known seaside town, a resort of summer tourists, some distance off, passed her in quick succession. She walked on for about two miles: then, hot and weary, choked with dust, she gave up in despair.

"He won't come," she thought, and she turned back.

All her spirits were gone. It served her right, she told herself; she had done wrong. She had been unfaithful to William. After all, he was going to marry her; why should she be running after another man? And even putting William aside, why should she be running after a man?

Stephen's motor was coming along behind her. His man was driving, and he was gazing down the unattractive roadway, thinking of her. He watched a tall woman ahead who walked as if she was tired.

She reminded him of Pen. The car shot by in a cloud of dust and then stopped. It was Pen.

"You go on home, Dodd," said Stephen. "I shall walk the rest of the way."

They met face to face, and the surprise on his side, and the reaction from disappointment on hers, had the effect of making the meeting much more warm than it otherwise would have been. If there was any ice left to be broken, this meeting broke it. These two, who had not seen each other more than three times in their lives, met with the openness and familiarity of lovers, or of those who share a secret. They laughed in each other's eyes; they seemed to be resuming a conversation. She gave him her hand; he held it a little and she did not seem even surprised.

As they rambled, he called her attention to various features of the country in sight. What she saw was the keen, unflinching eyes of the man beside her; the temples with the veins showing, on one of which a strip of bleached hair about the breadth of a finger shot with singular effect among the black; the rather full lips and steady chin; and a certain air of distinction, of quality and importance, which he owed to a fairly long line of ancestors who had managed to get things their own way and keep them there.

"Haven't you been to Gillingford?" he was asking. She turned to him laughing happily, and he was captivated by the sudden coloration of this pale countenance under the lightest, most fugitive impression. He loved the occasional audacity of her look, and the capacity for passionate love (arising from cerebral and nervous instigation, self-suggestion, more than from any germinal instinct), revealed by the slightest gestures of the girl, by her whole attitude, by the incessant neurotic agitation which might be inferred from her sensitive face.

"Gillingford is worth seeing. There is a fine old church, ruins of an abbey, one or two other sights. The streets are very quaint and picturesque. Why not come over on Friday?"

An insect had lit on her neck and she did not seem able to get rid of it. She stopped in the road smiling distressfully, her fingers groping about her throat.

"I can't get it off," she said.

She felt his long fingers touching her neck, his face was very near her own. Then the fly was captured, and they walked on rather silent, till they came to the first houses of Palebrook.

"Why not come on Friday?" he repeated.

"Well. ..." She hesitated and kicked a stone along the road. Then she turned, smiling. "I don't know that it would be quite what they call the thing, would it? This is such a little gossipy place."

She said that to say something. At this moment she was resolved to go.

"Oh, the thing!" He looked at her persuasively. "I tell you what you've got to do. If you're afraid the Palebrookites will think we're eloping, just stroll along the road and I'll pick you up as I pass. Most natural thing in the world."

The touch of intrigue appealed to her. "Don't count on me," she said, still smiling.

"Of course not!" he protested. "About eleven on Friday morning, you know." And upon that they separated.

Pen hurried back, and burst into Mrs. Wrench's parlour. "Oh, mother darling, I do hope you haven't missed me."

"Common marriage," said William.

He was sitting there in flannels playing bezique with her mother. He had evidently come straight up from the boating-party. Pen's heart smote her. While she was with another man—yes, and arranging a tryst with him, William had been thinking of her all the time in the midst of his pleasures. He must love her furiously. She would have to marry him, after all. From this evening, good-bye, Ruggles!

"Have you been anywhere special?" asked the young man.

Had he seen her? Was this the voice of suspicion? Pen was a little confused, and pretended to be setting her hair straight before the glass.

"Only a general canter. Why do you ask?"

William had not the least notion why he had asked, so he did not answer.

"Mother, I met Mr. Ruggles," Pen brought out. This was to salve her conscience with William.

"He's your great friend, isn't he?" asked William, but in a tone that no vanity, however acute, could distinguish from the flaccid accents in which he was declaring his cards. "He has given ours the shake. Aunt Laura thought he was in London."

Aunt Laura's name generally affected Pen like a scrubbing-brush on a tender skin, and if anything could increase her admiration for Ruggles it was to hear of his slight to the Burger connection. But alas!

that was all over. Poor old William—there he was pining for her, so much in love with her that he quitted the elements of gaiety to come and play bezique with her mother, in restless anxiety for her appearance. He might seem harsh, bouncing, over-bearing, but what a heart of gold! She covered the young man with attentions; she listened submissively, and acquiesced when he laid down his opinions on matters which she thought she knew as much about as he did, and perhaps more; she actually embarrassed him with her tendernesses.

"I must be off," he said. "It's as much as my life is worth to be late for dinner. I shan't have many more days of good dinners. My time is nearly up. I suppose you'll be going back to London too?"

As soon as he said it he saw his error. Of course she would insist on their engagement being declared before they left Palebrook. He waited for her to say it. But she said nothing of the kind.

Far from it! The one thing she wanted now was to keep the engagement dark. What would Stephen think of her when he learned that all this time she had been engaged? Oh, thrice cursed engagement! Oh, folly! Oh, spiteful fortune! And she had been calmly planning to go to Gillingford. She must be crazy. If William only didn't love her! She watched his back up the street, the lovelorn man. It occurred to her that she had watched the other like that. ...

But William was striding through the town, panic-stricken. "She's madly in love with me. She gave the whole show away just now. She'll never give up the engagement of her own accord. Oh, damn it all! If she had only stayed in London! But in this hole she has no one to think of but me, and that has made her worse. Oh, damn it all! I shall have to marry her just the same. Good-bye, Sabina."

And Pen sat staring at her shoes. "Mother," she said after a bit, "you know Ruggles?"

"Yes, dear; I have heard you mention him once or twice."

"Well, we met on purpose this afternoon. I've been with him alone for over an hour!"

"So that's what kept you out! I was wondering what you had found to do."

When a man prepares a bomb with incredible skill and patience, and then anxiously explodes it, and after a most successful explosion, when the dust has settled, the operator hears the person his bomb was intended to blow through the roof remark sleepily: "I thought I heard a door bang somewhere in the house, but I may be mistaken"—the exploder may be excused if he feels a little hurt. Pen had put all her energy into what seemed to her a most startling announcement, a congeries of her scruples, and her mother sat on placid, soporific.

"You don't seem to understand," she insisted. "I've been with him alone."

"Yes; I know I wasn't with you."

"A fly got on my neck. I could have got it off if I'd liked, but I wanted him to help. And he did. Was there any harm in that?"

"No, I shouldn't think so." The mother looked more and more sleepy. "The fly had to be got off somehow."

"Yes. I should have thought a lot about it if I hadn't told you at once. Even when it was going on, I meant to tell you. Now I feel all right about it. But I don't think you quite realize the rest. I often wonder I'm your daughter. We're not a bit alike, are we? He wants me to motor to Gillingford with him on Friday. How does that strike you?"

The mother judged this worth looking at with some degree of seriousness. "Well, perhaps it might be better not. William mightn't like it."

"H'm. That's just what I thought." Pen kissed her mother. "You are a darling. Can I do anything for you, mother? Shall I bring you a cup of warm milk when you are in bed? I'm not a bit tired."

"She means to go," thought the mother. She had long ago found that whenever Pen intended to ignore her advice, or was acting against her in any way, she was always particularly sweet with her.

Chapter XX

FOR THE NEXT TWO days this amiability overflowed upon everybody. Mrs. Wrench, the girl Gertie, even Mrs. Wrench's boy, whom Pen had hitherto treated in a way that people who have not experienced the attitude of blacks in the coloured zone call "like a nigger," were delighted with her consideration and benevolence. Pen was living in a kind of tormented happiness. She turned over and over in her mind the incidents of her walk on Tuesday. She was haunted by the memory of Stephen. Still, she did not mean to go to Gillingford—at least she thought not. But she knew that at their last encounter he had quitted her upon a sort of understanding that she would meet him.

On Wednesday night she lay awake for hours, debating. The night-light shed phantoms on the walls and ceiling. She could hear the heavy breathing of some one who slept in the next room. Foot falls sounded in the street, becoming fewer and fewer, till at last the steps of one person walking struck sharply; a laugh, a far-off call, the scream of a railway whistle, a dog barking, a door banged—and then the little town sank to rest, with nothing to stir the silence but the church clock tolling the hours. Once a motor whizzed by: could it be his? She got out of bed and looked through the window. Nothing but the blank faces of the houses; that melancholy sight, shops closed in a benighted town with all the apparatus of custom, signs and posters, still conveying a message which nobody is there to heed; a flickering gas-lamp throwing a pool of light on the roadway. It was like seeing a body without a soul, or the clothes of one who is dead. She crept back into the blankets and longed for the morning—for life. She would not go to Gillingford. Stephen loved her; she was sure he loved her. Perhaps he would suffer terribly when he found she was not at the trysting-place. And this thought filled her eyes with tears.

On Thursday night she took three of her veronal tablets and slept a stifled sleep. When Mrs. Wrench brought her breakfast, she heard it was raining and rather cold. Then of course she could not go. He would not even expect her.

At about half-past ten she decided to take a walk out on the Gillingford road. That could do no harm, and she felt the need of fresh air. She would take an umbrella, but no coat, so even if she met the motor she could not go in it.

"I shall be back soon," she said to her mother.

"Then you are not going to Gillingford?"

"Of course not. I told you I should not go."

The mother raised her eyebrows and looked at the fire which had been lighted.

"Mother, how horrid of you! I believe you think I am going."

"No," said the mother. "But I'll expect you when I see you."

Pen left the house indignant. She had a good mind to go back to the room and sit there all day to prove that her mother was wrong; and it says much for the attraction Stephen exercised that she did not yield to this suggestion of perverse self-torture, so consonant with her nature.

Out on the Gillingford road, the wind, swooping across the plain, bent her umbrella and thrust her skirt between her legs, and progress was difficult. The rain plashed down with a different sound as the wind blew or lulled; a soaked horse looked reproachfully over a hedge; on either side, above lonely fields, the grey rain could be seen riding on the wind. Not a soul was in sight. "He will never expect me in this weather," she thought.

Ere she had gone half a mile, a motor, going slowly, came upon her unawares from a side road, and squished up beside her in the mud. Stephen jumped out.

"That's all right!" he cried. "I had almost given you up,—weather and all, you know. Get in."

She turned round, and he saw the woollen cap she wore pulled down close over her head, her hair blowing about, her face tinged with colour and wet with the rain.

"Oh, I'm not going," she said. "I can't. I have no coat."

"Nonsense. Of course you're going. I thought of the coat." And from the car he dragged a man's travelling coat.

That decided the question for Pen. If there was a coat there, already waiting for her, she must be intended to go. All her scruples evaporated as she went tearing through the country, at a rate which the long straight road encouraged, with the rain in her face.

"How lovely!" cried Pen; and Stephen, guessing she was one of those organizations which are inebriated by speed, went faster and faster, till out of the mist in the valley Gillingford steeple leaped up before them.

Pen was entrancing at Gillingford. She felt astonishingly well: she had that sort of warm content and well-being which comes to a woman who is acting in perfect harmony with her nature, and is indeed a sign that she is so acting. She cast herself on the stream of her sensations and let herself for once go freely, without a single terrified look at the hobgoblins which her imagination usually descried on the banks throwing lines to entangle her. To be in a strange town, unknown, she always found a stimulating experience; to be there with a man manifestly in love with her and of whom she was becoming fond, to be moving about by his side in the low-browed uncertain weather, their lives for the moment narrowed down to themselves, was all profit to her. And what told with her as much as anything else was the recollection that all this was momentary, a point taken in defiance of the laws of the game. It is, after all, a very elementary psychonomy which gives two people, whom you wish to make fall in love with each other, full liberty and opportunity, and to throw them, as the phrase is, into each other's arms; for it is in difficulty, in snatching a sip from the chalice in the teeth of fortune, that love waxes fiery. The fabulists who surrounded the enchanted princess with labyrinths and ferocious dragons, did but express this in pretty allegory. And so, when Mrs. Ford of Palebrook, who looks upon Tugg, the great athlete, as an ineligible suitor, whisks dear Jessie round the corner when she sees him afar in the street, she is doing just what she tries to provide against; for dear Jessie's half-turn and the sympathetic fluttering of handkerchiefs between her and Tugg, do more to keep their hearts aglow than if they could be, like happier people, an hour by themselves in a garden. ...

At lunch at the hotel Pen passed condemnation on the claret. She explained that she had learned the value of wines on the Continent. Then they strolled forth again, lingering purposeless before shop-windows, their breaths mingling audaciously in the damp air. And where the street widened, they came upon the great church which stood black and menacing in the grey day, surrounded by its regiment of graves.

The church, never lightsome even when the sun was shining, was now gloomy and quite still. It was empty, and their voices sounded hollow under the great oak-wroughten roof. Agitated at finding himself thus alone with her, he no longer tried to conceal the love in his eyes, but studied her mobile face avidly, longing to kiss her on the lips.

"If I do," he thought, "it means marriage."

As for her, she moved along, a little self-conscious perhaps, but very self-possessed, and showed a certain interest in the monuments. Her gloved hand hung down by her side, and he took it loosely in his own. She let it be so for a moment; then she gripped his hand firmly and pulled him after her to one of the chapels.

"Let us look at this," she said.

It was an ugly florid monument of the mid-eighteenth century. By an odd chance, his own name occurred in the Latin epitaph—the name of some ancestor of his, one Catherine Ruggles, married into a burgess family of Gillingford, long extinct. Pen's eye, glancing over the monument, lighted upon the name, and she drew away her hand.

"You are on your native heath here," she said pensively, a little wistfully.

"Yes, if that's anything."

The monument, which he had forgotten all about till this minute, interested him not at all. Why had she drawn away her hand?

"You are a dear!" she cried impulsively; and right in his face she flung the daring look she had given him once before at Palebrook.

It was too much. His arm was about her waist; he was seeking her lips; she held her head back with a tantalizing smile …

When a door banged, echoing footsteps sounded in the church, and a man coughed. It was the garage-man from the hotel, who had been ordered to bring the car round to the church at half-past three, and was now come to tell them it was outside.

They drove out of Gillingford very silent, nor did either of them try to go back on what had passed. Such little talk as they had was upon the incidents of the route.

"If it had not been for the garage-man," Ruggles was thinking, "I should have proposed to her then and there. Possibly he has handed me four thousand a year."

"If it had not been for the garage-man," Pen was thinking, "he would have proposed to me and I should have accepted him, William or no William. Possibly the garage-man has saved me a row, for William loves me desperately, I believe."

When they parted at Palebrook it was with an almost imperceptible shade of constraint. Pen ran in and woke her mother out of a nap.

"Here I am back, mother," she said and kissed her. "Were you anxious?"

"Oh no. You are so used to going about. You look rather tired. Did you enjoy it?"

"I enjoyed *myself*," said Pen slowly, "which is a different thing. That doesn't happen to me often, and it may never happen to me again."

Chapter XXI

THAT EVENING, RUGGLES GAVE his career the most drastic survey it had ever received. He was a man of a determined ambition, and to this hour he had thought it a cold ambition, which steadily cleared out of the road whatever stood in its way, and of all obstacles considered love the least. In fact, whenever he estimated the forces which might hinder him, love with its satellites was not even counted in. Any man, he thought, who allowed love to get such power over him that it set his plans awry and led him to choose solutions disadvantageous, was essentially a weak man who had no business with ambition. Yet here he was now, carried so far afield by love that it was doubtful if he would ever get back to the old road again. He was staring at the wall as if he saw written on it that there were some things to his great advantage which he felt the utmost reluctance to do, because they meant that he must lose Pen.

The Electoral Committee of his party had invited him a few days before to contest the Division, upon the imminent retirement of the sitting Member to the House of Lords. He had not yet sent any reply, although he knew that these gentlemen of the Committee were awaiting it with impatience. If he remained single he might agree to stand; or if he married Sabina. If he married Pen, the expense was more than he cared to face. Of course, to be a Member of Parliament nowadays was a much cheaper thing—cheaper in all ways—than it had been in his father's time; but this was one of the expensive Divisions, bristling with subscription lists, and what was worse, crowded with well-to-do people who always out of a spirit of emulation gave large subscriptions; and the present member, being an enormously wealthy coal-mine-owning Welsh baronet, they had got into the habit of seeing their member's name figuring near the top of all the lists. And there were other expenses, not only local, attached to the position when it was held by a man supposed to be rich and expected to forego the official salary for the benefit of charities in the constituency.

Nor was he sure that Pen would be of much assistance to him from a worldly point of view. He always had the power of stripping any object presented to him of all glamorous accessories which passion might cast upon it, and viewing it in a hard, cold light. However much he loved and admired Pen himself, he was aware that she might not go down in Palebrook; and it was essential that his wife should go down in Palebrook. The indefiniteness of her past, the fact that she lived obscurely in London, would be against her with the Palebrookites of one kind; her manner, call it foreign or what you will—anyhow, her whole attitude and way of doing things, with the other kind, the Mrs. Wrench kind. He freely acknowledged that Pen had appeared at her worst to everybody but himself since she had been here; the stupid behaviour of Spring, and the coldness of that youth's relations, placing

the sensitive creature in what she was sure to look upon as an equivo-
cal position, setting her on the defensive, and sterilizing social powers
which were, he thought, considerable. Nay, he could discern in her a
reserve power of the noble art of "getting on" with its accessories, a
knack of picking out the "right people" to know, and the rest, which
had not hitherto developed—or only in the wrong directions—from
lack of a wide enough field to exercise in, and might be quite as for-
midable as anything in that line Palebrook had to offer. But even so,
however useful her gifts, she would have to fight against a serried hostility at Palebrook which it might take her years to wear down, and be
the more difficult to tackle because it would not be obvious—there was
nobody in Palebrook who would dare to be rude to his wife—but con-
sist rather of things left undone than of things done.

Sabina, on the other hand, would be heartily welcomed; there was
nothing about her at all to jar, and the immense wealth of her father
would be of itself a letter of credit: she would be "a dear little thing" for
one side, and "a nice quiet little lady" for the other. But there would be
no joy in a marriage with Sabina; it would be hard business; the epitha-
lamium would be written in a ledger. Certainly four thousand a year
was a good thing; but between him and that interposed the vision of
the long Pen presiding at his dinner-table with her four languages and
selections from Schubert. She would be far more impressive to people
in general married than single; far less restless, far more urbane and
assured. True, she would always have her moods; it would always need
a certain management to live with her in comfort; but Sabina, he suspected, might develop in intimacy moods far more trying than Pen's,
without Pen's generous, impulsive nature to neutralize them.

The result of all this balancing was a project singularly weak for a man
usually so determined and sure of himself. He had indeed struck it
out as he dawdled over breakfast on the following Monday morning,
in complete despair of arriving at any conclusion more definite. What
he thought was, that if he could have Sabina in front of him while
he debated with himself, he would know better where he stood. He
resolved to see her that afternoon.

Before starting, he slipped into his pocket the copy of *Poems and
Ballads.* He did not quite know what use he intended to make of it, or

whether he intended to make any use of it at all; but a situation might arise where it would be useful.

"The Firs," as he came up to it, had that unmistakable look of country-houses on a summer day when everybody is out. The doors and windows stood open; stillness reigned, broken only by the cooing of doves and the sound of a laugh far at the back. Instead of ringing, he strolled round to the side of the house to see if by chance anybody was on the lawn. Then, finding no one, as the long window of the drawing-room stood wide open, he passed through it, and as he did so it came upon him that it was there he had first surrendered to the witchery of Pen on a night of flowers and stars. Wherever the philtre had been brewed, in what dim hall of fate, it was on this spot it had touched his lips. And he was so profoundly moved that he walked into the middle of the room without perceiving Sabina till she called him by name.

She was dressed in white, with a black sash, and a bunch of red flowers in the sash. She was totally unoccupied, and had been either asleep or day-dreaming till he came in. She was sunk far back in the deep chair, and her shoes hung some distance above the floor like those of a child of twelve.

"I thought everybody was out," he said.

"Everybody is out," replied Sabina, "but me. Laura went out driving after lunch, Mr. Burger is gone over to Ventnor, and Mr. Spring is playing tennis at the Fords'. I didn't go anywhere, because we were awfully late at the Parrys' last night and I wanted to rest."

Her prim, monotonous voice had lost some of its cordiality.

"I should think Mr. Spring will be in soon," she added, colouring faintly.

Why should she colour? For a moment he wondered whether she was in love with Spring. If so, his debate was over; he had only to pick up his hat and go; Sabina and her four thousand a year could be put out of his calculations. Her next remark, however, did not seem to bear out this theory.

"You have taken to a solitary life, haven't you? You haven't been seen or heard. Laura thought you had disappeared." She spoke with some little irritation.

"Absconded with my clients' funds," said Ruggles, whose humour had a professional tinge.

"I don't know what you mean," replied Sabina, who had no humour at all. "I suppose my horse is still lame?"

"Quite lame." He thought he was not doing it well, not putting his heart into it as if he wanted to win. "I've been very much occupied of late." Then he tried to find out just where he was. "But no doubt Mr. Spring has been keeping my memory green."

Sabina raised her eyebrows and her mouth twitched a little. "Keeping your memory green?"

"I mean, he has been taking my place for the outdoor exercise. As he is in the house here he ought to be able to do that. He can't always be wrapped up in poetry."

She glanced down and began turning a bracelet round her large wrist which was out of proportion to the rest of her frame. "Mr. Spring is very nice. Everybody says he is tremendously clever."

"Do they?"

"Yes; except you, I think. But then you told me that you didn't care for poetry."

Ruggles pulled his book half out of his pocket. "I can't take it as daily bread," he laughed, "but I appreciate a good thing."

"Then you ought to like Mr. Spring's poetry. I don't profess to understand it all myself, but he's repeated it so often now that I'm getting quite into it. He has started some new kind of thing now. It sounds just like a piece out of the newspaper, but of course it is poetry really. Mr. Spring told me it is easier to remember than the other kind."

"Ah," said Ruggles. "That would count with him, no doubt."

"Yes. The vicar was telling me at dinner the other night that he considered it real genius, and that Mr. Spring ought to publish his poetry. The vicar's opinion is worth having. He's a critic. He writes for the Reviews."

Ruggles thought: "And yet he doesn't know Swinburne when he hears it;" but he kept his thought to himself. He assented vaguely, and felt for his book as a man put on his defence feels for his revolver. Now was his time to explode Spring.

"What is your book?" asked Sabina, smiling for the first time—perhaps because she noticed his agitation and put it down to the right side of the account.

"Only a book of poetry."

"Poetry? I shouldn't have thought you had the least poetry about you."

A vision of a rainy day, a gloomy church, and a tall pale girl with a white woollen cap pulled down over her amber hair standing by a monument, while her exquisite voice poured through lips which smiled triumphant love, and also a touch of love's sorrow, came before his eyes. What was he doing here, far away from her heart and the touch of her slender, imperial hands? How had he deluded himself that he could forget her?

Sabina was following some thought of her own. "Laura ought to be in soon"—she glanced at the clock—"or her nephew. By the by," she pursued, "do you know anything of those friends of Mr. Spring's, the Hazards?"

For once the lawyer's masterly self-possession was almost shaken. He actually looked a little confused.

"Oh, I know them, as you may say—" He completed the phrase with a gesture.

"My own acquaintance with them is very slight. Miss Hazard is rather an overwhelming person, I find." Sabina's blunt little face was bent down. "But I believe they are great friends of Mr. Spring. I've sometimes wondered if he and Miss Hazard were engaged."

Engaged! She engaged to Spring! Stephen could hardly contain himself. She was his! He knew it by a thousand signs. The duplicity of women was fathoms deep, but no woman could act as Pen had acted with him when she was in love with another man. That was not in nature. One thing was certain: Spring should not have her—not if he could help it. And he could help it. Spring might have Sabina and four thousand a year, or forty thousand, but he should not have Pen, by God!

He rammed the book far down in his pocket. "It is not in the least true," he said with his most incisive voice and his hard, glittering smile. "I have the best reasons for knowing there is nothing of the kind."

She looked up, rather surprised. "Really? I somehow thought—of course, if *you* know—You know everything that goes on in Palebrook, don't you? Laura will be glad. I don't think she wants her nephew to marry Miss Hazard."

"Well, he won't. She can make her mind easy on that score." And with that he rose to go away.

"Does this mean we are going to see some more of you?" said Sabina. "I'm afraid I must go home at the end of next week."

"I was fortunate to find you," he parried. "I really came up to borrow a newspaper. Mine have gone astray—Bank holiday, you know. I wanted to look up the international crisis."

"I never pay attention to such stupid things," said Sabina. "I've given up newspapers. There has been nothing in them lately but the stupid old Servians. How uninteresting!"

She held out her hand, and as he took it he thought, "There's four thousand a year gone!" It was a last tribute to that old life, the life devoted exclusively to his own interest, which lay dying at his feet. He was never to see it alive again.

As soon as she was alone, Sabina walked over to a mirror and stood gazing at herself. "If he was ever going to propose to me, he would have done it this afternoon. He never will now."

She sighed, because she wanted to marry. Seeing her fortune, she could have easily found many a man eager to marry her; but she wanted a man, as she often said, whom she could love.

Chapter XXII

R UGGLES HAD NOT BEEN gone many minutes when William came in. Sabina heard his harsh voice in the hall talking to the maid.

"They're all out, I suppose. Is there anything to drink in the house?"

"Oh, yes, sir."

"Well, I don't want any slops. Get me some hock and seltzer."

With the tumbler in his hand he came into the drawing-room. "Hullo," he cried, "I thought everybody was out. Lord, I'm thirsty."

Standing in the middle of the room, he raised the long tumbler to his lips and gurgled the contents down his throat, without pausing till he came to the last drop. Then he drew a deep breath. Sabina gazed at him in admiration. It was a fine performance.

"Pah!" said William, his ejaculation being something between a word and a snort. "I could do another of those. I never was so thirsty, ab-so-lute-ly never. I must have a fever or something."

"Did you have a good game?" Sabina inquired.

"Rotten. A rotten lot there too. How those Fords find out all the feeble slackers they get to their place, I simply can't make out. They dispute every blessed ball. It's all well enough, but—I mean, you must draw the line somewhere."

He flung himself into a chair; stuffed his hands into the pockets of his white flannel trousers, stretched out his long legs, and stood his pipe-clayed shoes on heel, with some inches of pink sock showing above them. His sun-browned neck was bare to the collar-bone; his chin was plunged down in the collar of his crimson "blazer;" a cloud rested sulkily on his handsome face. He felt himself very badly treated. He had this morning received a letter from Ibed's, refusing peremptorily an extension of holiday he had applied for. He had, besides, seen Ruggles leaving the house as he approached. Ruggles, he supposed, was here to make love to Sabina; they might even have arranged to have the house to themselves. In that case all his trouble, his poetry and so on, was wasted.

What damnable luck was his! Why couldn't he have a shot at the four thousand a year? There were two barriers—Ruggles and Penelope. Sabina, perhaps, was in love with Ruggles; Penelope insisted upon being in love with him. He might do for Ruggles in some way; he felt himself equal to the lawyer; but what manoeuvre would avail against Penelope? It was very hard; and he stared at the carpet in a state of grave depression. He hoped Sabina would keep silent; he didn't feel equal to talking all that literary rot just now.

She on her part made no attempt to break the silence: she had far too much respect for the meditations of the poet. That his meditations were gloomy, even tragic, his face betrayed. It reminded her vaguely of portraits of Byron. She admired him thus; the eyes which she kept on his profile had some ardour; every fibre of her little body was sympathetic to the tall, muscular frame before her.

Propinquity is what counts in generating love: supposing the affections not already deeply engaged, the man on the spot has an enormous advantage. That wise woman, Aunt Laura, had probably remembered this axiom when she asked William and Sabina to her house together. Sabina had been sentimental about Ruggles, and if her sentiment had been encouraged it might well have blossomed into love; but she had never seen anything like so much of Ruggles at one time as she had seen lately of William. And then, suddenly, Ruggles had withdrawn altogether, neglecting her. This did more for William than all Aunt Laura's machinations, for it threw Sabina in a sort of pique on the nearest man she found congenial.

William she found congenial; what is more, she admired him; and just there was her difficulty. She was in fact rather in awe of him. She could not imagine that towering intellect bending to the frivolities of love; still less, occupied with the little duties of the domestic relation. It would be like eating your breakfast with Solomon in all his glory. Up to now their intercourse had mainly consisted in William laying down the law on every subject broached and Sabina meekly accepting it—a situation which William found extremely flattering and agreeable and Sabina not disagreeable, for she considered herself lucky to be in the way of hearing words of wisdom from such a man, and moreover, she enjoyed looking at the sage's fresh-coloured face.

She enjoyed it now, though she was a little hurt by his prolonged silence. "He does not think me worth talking to," she thought. "He believes I am not capable of sharing his ideas." At last she said innocently: "I suppose it is at this hour that you think over your poetry?"

It was as if a wasp had stung him. "Oh bother!" he cried peevishly. "I'm sick of all that."

The moment they were spoken he wished he could recall the words. He had gone too far. Still, after all, there was not much use in keeping up the game any longer. He had to go back to Ibed's, and he was engaged to be married.

"The fact is that a man isn't always in condition for that kind of thing," he amended lamely.

He looked at Sabina with some defiance, expecting to find her shocked. On the contrary, she was radiant. She had just learned that he did not insist upon being always on the heights; he could come down to her level—nay, he was apparently willing to remain at her level if she would but allow him. She was to blame for always trying to keep their conversations up in such a rarefied atmosphere; and Heaven knows how it tried her to do so! But what longanimity he had shown! How much more intimate they might have been by now if she had only guessed that the great mind needed relaxation, and was only very glad to accommodate itself to the small things of existence.

"I should fancy it would be rather dangerous to keep it up continually," she ventured. "It is too much mental strain."

William caught at this eagerly. "You're absolutely right. That's just what it is: I've found it out myself. Too much mental strain. Supposing people were married," he added jocosely, "they couldn't go on talking poetry all day. Perfectly impossible. It would be too wearing."

Sabina coloured—she coloured for very little—and began twisting her rings. Really, she felt more at ease with him than she had ever done before; and as he dropped down from the height to which she had imaginatively hoisted him, she was able to contemplate him as the ordinary, handsome man, and his physical advantages began to appeal to her for the first time at their full value, unhindered. If Ruggles had now produced his book, the effect would have been certainly null. William added to the effect he was producing by hinting jealousy.

"I thought I saw Ruggles up here just now."

"Yes. He imagined we were all out and came to get a newspaper from the servants. Not a friendly visit, I'm afraid," she laughed. "He said he wanted to see about the war."

"What war?"

"I'm sure I don't know. Some ridiculous crisis in Europe or Africa or somewhere. I thought *you* could tell me," said she with flattering deference.

"There is no war," said William decisively. "I know the war I'd like to see though. We'll jolly well have to lick the Germans some day. Those brutes ought to be called down."

"I know so few Germans," she said.

"I meet them in the city. Awful swine." An unpleasant recollection shadowed his face. "In two days I shall be in London." He brought it out dismally. "Swotting."

"And I shall be back in Manchester. How strange everything is! It seems such a coincidence."

The house was quite still; the long shadows were creeping over the grass; it was the hour of lovers, and it emboldened William.

"We have a lot in common," he said, and looked at her tenderly, though he had no definite purpose in his head beyond a little flirting to rouse her interest and assuage his baffled soul. How could he go further? He was a trammelled man.

"I have often thought that," murmured Sabina with a little sigh.

William's look of tenderness increased. She was really not half bad, he thought. She was rather pretty. "I shall miss our talks, I know that."

"Yes?" She seemed pleased. "It has been nice for me. I haven't much to look forward to at home. I don't get on there somehow, and I haven't many friends—not real friends. Nobody tries to make things pleasant for me."

William had heard from Uncle Herbert that old Moll complained bitterly that Sabina upset the house from cellar to garret when she was at home, and that everybody was glad when she decided to go on a visit. But as he had formed the lowest opinion of old Moll, he respected her for not being able to get on with her father; and he recognized that he himself must be pretty high in her favour for her to make these confidences. So he shoved his hands deeper in his pockets, looked indignant, and murmured, "Beastly shame."

"Father says——" Sabina hesitated. Then she came out with it in the tone of one relating an insult she has suffered, for which she expects condolence: "Father says that I ought to marry."

The impulse to polygamy is strong in men. It overcame William now. Forgetting Pen and his engagement, he got up and went over to Sabina. "Then why not marry me?"

She looked at him with parted lips and startled eyes. She was astonished; she had really not expected it. But William, with the admirable instinct of the unintellectual male, who perceives the inefficacy of talk as compared to contact in these matters, knelt down and took her in his arms.

That settled it. It was the first time in her experience, and she was overpowered. "I love you," whispered Sabina shyly.

"Darling!" said William, giving her a hug of such vigour that it nearly pulled her out of the chair. "There will be a devil of a row over this!" he thought.

"Do you love me, William?" she asked.

Again scorning words, he gave her another hug, and this time she found that she could maintain her position more conveniently on her feet.

"Then why do you look so sad?" She smiled softly.

"Mum, mum, mum!" William made these incoherent noises with his mouth full of some of the stuff of her blouse, which he had taken a bite of at the shoulder. "Not sad. Naughty to say sad. Not sad at all."

As Sabina could not lean her head on his shoulder in the classical attitude, she leant her head on his elbow and looked into his eyes. "Well, worried then. And I think I know why."

"If you do," thought William, "I'll be shot."

"You are afraid that father will object to you because—well, because you are a junior clerk."

It had not occurred to him before, but now that it was stated he felt it was what one might well expect from old Moll's general beastliness. A man who didn't believe in tips wouldn't be likely to know a decent son-in-law when he saw one.

"Now I'll tell you what we must do," Sabina went on prettily. "We must say you are awfully eager to work."

William's face clouded.

Sabina saw the danger and tacked. "Oh, I don't mean like you are at Ibed's. Father must find you a big position in his works. He'll do that. He's so anxious to have me married. And then you are Laura's nephew. That's a great advantage. She has heaps of influence with him. She'll talk him round."

William kissed her with the same kind of enthusiasm as that of a man who drinks a toast in cold water. His fears were not allayed by any means. But Sabina's kiss came from her soul on the lips of the handsome youth.

"I used to think," she said in a low voice, "—wasn't it silly?—that you were engaged to Miss Hazard."

He was staggered, but he countered neatly. "Oh, I say, how about you and Stephen Ruggles?"

Sabina looked into space and smiled and sighed, and then clung to the tall specimen of manhood before her. William wished she were not so small; he had really to bend almost double. ...

Then he thought of the extremely pointed letter he was now in a position to send Ibed, and he was consoled.

Two little cats, dozing in chairs, began to amuse themselves. This athletic love-making drew them from their phlegm. They had seen many things, but this scene of a very long man and a very short woman hauling each other about was exceptional. They were so curious that they drew near, and one of them humorously planted her nails in William's ankle. William kicked; the black cat fled out of the window, while the white cat rolled on the floor and laughed with her little pink mouth. ...

⁂

A few moments later, Aunt Laura stood in the window. The lovers were sitting close together. She took in the scene and judged it. Then she walked carelessly into the room.

"I'm frightfully hot," she said, "and *tired!* Sabina, dear, I hope you don't think me too rude for words not to have come back sooner. But I've been so rushed! You can't imagine what it has been."

She went on talking to give them a chance to regain their composure.

"It's not very hot," contradicted William, to cover his awkwardness. "It's rather cool."

"Isn't it?" put in Sabina, her face flushed.

"Well," said Aunt Laura, "I'm sure I am glad you find it so."

Then, without hurrying or making any excuse, still as it were keeping in contact with the conversation of the others, she picked up the white kitten and strolled away again out into the garden.

There was an odd look on her face—pleasure, tinged with a vague, charming irony.

"I've brought it off," she said to herself. "How funny!"

Chapter XXIII

"I CAN'T EAT," SAID PEN, fretfully shoving her chair back from the table. "I hate cold supper."

She lit a cigarette, and stood leaning against the mantelpiece while she smoked, looking very discouraged.

"I don't seem to be able to help myself, do I, mother? I do these things simply, you know, without thinking, and then I go through torments after. But he had no right to take advantage of me." She paused and frowned. "He was trying to ruin my life."

"Oh, that's an exaggeration," said the mother impatiently. She had her querulous moods as well as her daughter, and besides, the vicar had called on her that afternoon and she was now undergoing a spasm of acute respectability. "But I warned you not to go to Gillingford. It was throwing yourself in his way. I don't call that behaviour for a girl. If a man wanted me I'd make him come and find me."

"Mother!" Pen's eyes filled with tears. "How can you say such cruel things to me!"

Probably because she was really in love, the stupid platitudes stung her like a discharge of pins. They were an appeal to that unstable religiosity, the weariness of all her youth in its most ineffectual conflict with her pagan nature, which it could only make turbid since it was not powerful enough to dam up the undercurrent of longing for a liberal life, facile and direct, without second thoughts. She took out her handkerchief to wipe her eyes.

Her mother looked at her relentlessly. "What are you crying about? You make me scold you because you tire me out with your eternal complaints. It never occurs to you that I have feelings as well as you. Here I've listened to nothing since last night but how that man squeezed your hand and tried to kiss you, and whether you were to blame or not. What pleasure do you think I can have in listening to all that? You wait till you have a daughter of your own and see how you'll enjoy it."

"But you told me that you liked to hear things," sobbed Pen. "I shall never tell you another word."

Mrs. Hazard picked up the poker and dabbed viciously at the small fire. "Very well; that will be so much gained. I wish to goodness if you're going to marry William that you'd hurry up and do it, instead of dawdling about after other men."

At this Pen stopped crying. "Why are you so anxious that I should marry William?" she asked fiercely. "You know well enough that we shouldn't be happy together. You often say so. And yet there's not a day passes that you don't ask me when I'm going to marry him. I can't understand you."

The mother, who did not wish to confess her genuine reason, which was simply that she was sick of having a grown-up daughter about and accordingly welcomed anybody or anything that promised to take her away, fell back on silence while she collected a plausible reply.

"One would think you didn't care whether I was happy or not," said Pen.

This drove Mrs. Hazard from crossness to positive ill-temper. "I suppose you knew what you were about when you got engaged," she cried vehemently. "You're old enough, Heaven knows! I was married when I was twenty, and here you are twenty-six and still on the shelf—and likely to be, seeing the way you go on. If I'd had my way, I should have spoken to that Mrs. Burger as soon as we came down. That's what we came down for. But of course you knew best. Now you can settle your own business. All I say is, settle it somehow and have done with it."

"Oh, you are cruel," wailed Pen, sobbing afresh. "I can never think the same of you again. I used to love you so much too. I see now that all you want is to get rid of me. I'll look out for a place as governess or secretary, and go and live by myself as soon as we get back to London."

"You can go to-morrow if you like," snapped Mrs. Hazard. She lit a cigarette and puffed at it furiously, and opened *What Every Woman Ought to Know* at the chapter on the Ideal Home.

In the lull that followed, Mrs. Wrench's maid entered. To explain the opportunity of her arrival, it should be mentioned that she had come some little time before into the passage, but hearing voices raised in dispute she had carefully applied her ear to the keyhole and kept it there while the dramatic interest was at its height. Now she came forward holding a letter between her thumb and finger.

"Please, mum," she said, "it's for miss, and Mr. Ruggles' man is waiting."

Pen flushed scarlet. No one thing could have come more unseasonably on top of the discussion—no, not even Ruggles in person.

"All right, Gertie, you needn't wait. I'll give the man the answer myself." And Pen broke open the envelope.

Then, when the maid had left the room, "Do you want to read it?" she asked.

The mother kept her eyes obstinately on her book, but curiosity got the better of her and she held out her hand. A few lines were written lengthwise across the paper:

> *"I must see you to-morrow. It is most important. Please send appointment by bearer.—S. R."*

"H'm!" cried Mrs. Hazard, and tossed the note on the table. Her tone was a mixture of satire and contempt. "He seems pretty intimate. He doesn't even begin with your name."

"Do you think I had better make an appointment?" Pen spoke a little tremulously.

"I'm sure I can't tell you. If I mention William, you say I'm forcing him down your throat. But of course you'll see this man, say what I will."

"There you're wrong," exclaimed Pen, rising like a white flame. "I will not see him."

She snatched up Stephen's note and an envelope and swept out of the room. On the table in the passage there were a pen and ink, and she wrote across the face of his message: "I cannot. Good-bye."

As she was sticking down the envelope she paused. She had her handkerchief in her hand, a little rag of a thing damp with her tears, and after pondering a moment, she stuffed that in too. Then she gave the packet to the messenger and came back to the parlour.

"I think I shall go to bed." Her voice was husky, and she spoke with her head round the door.

"Very well," replied the mother frigidly.

"Are you very angry, mother, dear?"

"I am as well as can be expected," came the answer in a most uncompromising tone.

Pen sighed. "Good night," she said almost in a whisper.

There was no reply.

Chapter XXIV

RUGGLES WAS TRYING TO prolong his dessert after dinner, when the note came. He would have been more alarmed by her message, if it had not been for the handkerchief accompanying it. This stirred in him depths of tenderness which he had never suspected. The bit of cambric was crumpled and moist—perhaps with tears shed because they must part. It had still a faint perfume which he had noticed about her when they were together. Whatever the note meant, the handkerchief was an avowal most gracious, most tender, and he pressed it to his lips.

The note might simply mean that her mother, thinking he did not contemplate marriage, had forbidden her to see more of him; but he could not believe that Pen would allow matters to come to a halt on that account if the road were otherwise clear. It might mean that the relations with Spring were deeper and more obscure than he had supposed. Or it might even mean—for what did he know of her life?—that there was some other entanglement in London or elsewhere which would make a marriage with him impossible.

This thought he found so grievous that he could not rest still in the house, and he wandered out under the moon. It was a mild, windless night, and no sound could be heard from his terrace save the bleating of a flock of sheep folded far off on the lea. With that desire common to lovers to look upon the mere walls which house the beloved, he found himself strolling down to Palebrook. The High Street on this Bank-holiday night was filled with the townspeople and people come in from the country and over from the Isle of Wight, and he was too well known to parade up and down in front of Mrs. Wrench's windows. But at the back of the house there was a small garden which ran down to the canal, with a muddy lane at the foot of it. He could easily find his way in the moonlight.

Pen undressed and got into bed, but she could not sleep. She was like one who watches the dust arising just after a building has caved in. Her life, she thought, had sunk into ruin. She had put Stephen out of her life, and with him went her interest in life. Existence with her mother was become impossible. She would have to marry William, or as that seemed now almost beyond her power, the alternative was to begin again those deadly lessons, and live in cheap lodgings by herself. Or she might go out as a governess and be tolerated by a family. What a shame that she had only that to fall back on—she who loathed anything in the nature of an intellectual task and took no interest whatever in manifestations of the budding intelligence. Heavens, how grey and hopeless it all was! Oh, the grinding misery of being poor! And she had put Stephen out of her life. She turned on her pillow and began to cry again.

After a while she heard her mother come to bed, and some time after that the church clock struck ten. She got up and looked out of the window. The street was growing quieter. In a star-strewn sky the moon sailed gloriously through a stream of misty light. Her room seemed close, and she thought she would like to be out in the moonshine.

She remembered a back-door which led into the garden, easy to unlock. Thus she could breathe the night wind and the unwalled liberty of the night. She put on a loose dressing robe of white serge over her nightgown, and a long blue scarf which trailed down from her loosened hair. Then she lit a cigarette and descended.

The garden breathed faintly of blush pinks, honeysuckle and marjoram, and there was no sound at all in the garden. The rumour from the street came so softened as to blend into the general whisper of the night. The little wind was caressing, and Pen stretched her arms out full length, threw back her head, and breathed it in.

Now, as she stood thus, Stephen rose up from a low wall on which he had been sitting for some time, and glanced backward up the garden. He doubted the report of his eyes. It was an hallucination, a ghost in the moonshine. Then he saw a cigarette glowing in a long frail hand, with an odd, well-remembered curve of the little finger which he always used to think so personal and expressive.

He leaped from the wall and made up the lane to the wicket which opened on the garden, keeping his eyes all the time fixed on the tall, immobile white figure. Pen, hearing the click of the gate, started back and sent her gaze through the pale night. Something in her heart told her it was he, and she came forward at once with her lithe grace, laughing low in her throat she knew not why.

Of the pleasures of life, few exceed the pleasure of finding some one you love, whom you have lately parted from as you thought for years, or whom you believed to be at a distance, unexpectedly standing before you. It is one of the sweetest respites on our haggard march. At such a moment, if ever in a lifetime, the world is lost sight of with its fardels and trammels, and actions become genuine and sheer as the sunrise, or the surf rolling to the shore. It caused in these two a kind of delirium which made no case at all of the debates and prudences and hesitations they had of late found so heavy. He saw the little laugh in her eyes, the kind of glorious insouciance which the moment—one of her most splendid moments—gave her as she came down the path; and she saw the desire on his face and his arms held out. A force that she made no attempt to resist drew her towards him; and then she was in his arms, and he was kissing the creamy face and amber-coloured hair under the electric softness of the moon.

"At last!" he murmured. "How I have longed for this! I see now that this is the one thing I desired out of all the world."

"Oh!" she sighed helplessly. "Why did you come?"

"I came to ask you to marry me."

She quivered, opened her eyes and tried to get free.

"No, no," she moaned. "That is impossible. I can't."

He felt the softness of her soft garments under his arm, and held her closer.

"You can't? Ah, but you can, Pen; you must!" Thereupon a searing thought leaped through his head, but he held her still closer. "Why can't you? You are not married?"

"Oh no!" She struggled again to get free.

"Then nothing else counts," said Stephen, and he kissed her on the neck.

Pen covered his mouth with her hand. "Hush! I must go in now. I'll see you to-morrow and explain. It would be too hard to-night—after this!" She ran up the path and stood a second in the doorway, looking at him with a wonderful smile. "Darling!" she whispered, and shut the door.

On the other side of the door she paused before she went upstairs. "I wonder do I love him as much as that?" she asked herself.

When she was in bed she decided that she did.

Chapter XXV

RUGGLES LIT A CIGAR and strolled homeward through the vacant Palebrook street. At first he thought of nothing, and he read the familiar signs on the shops. The night, he thought, was very oppressive. Then, gradually, as he neared the top of the street, he realized that there lay on his mind a vague uneasiness. It was like the awakening in the morning after some drama overnight.

By degrees his reflections hardened into shape. He was now certain to marry her: she had declared she was not married, and nothing else must stand in the way. He would not tolerate anything else in the way. He could never love any one as he loved Pen.

This, however, did not prevent him from reviewing with harrowing lucidity what a marriage with her would mean. He saw her neurasthenia, her incalculable moods, her impulse to flirt with any man who attracted her, and the tiresome scene of remorse which would inevitably follow. He saw, furthermore, that she could never be absorbed in any group known to Palebrook: it was impossible to imagine her golfing, tennis-playing, hockey playing, like all the girls in the place, and their mothers too. People would have to make the best of her way of looking at life, for she would never come round to theirs. Once she was firmly settled, she would not care a farthing whether a thing was decreed to be done or not done by the Palebrook and county society: if she wanted to do it, do it she would. Her individuality might even tend to isolate her. Nevertheless, he felt that if he were deprived of her now, life would become without savour. Her very defects made her more dear.

He lived over again that glorious passionate minute in the garden, and he vowed that to have held her thus was worth a fragment of life. To hold her again like that was surely worth a life. It would seem as if he had been struck by a ray of this wonderful moon—the kind of moon old witches choose to gather their simples under. He was lifted to summits he had never dreamed of touching in his wildest flights before. For this experience he was willing to risk a thousand disenchantments, if disenchantments must be. And he too, the hard-and-fast lawyer, knew the touch of rapture, and shared an hour with Mark Antony and the other great lovers of the world. There, in the prosaic Palebrook street, to which only the moonbeams lent a touch of romance, he found himself, somewhat to his own astonishment, asking what more is to be gained in the whole world after one has had love, the real love, the love of her for whose embrace the lover is willing to die. ...

As he turned into the Avenue it became somewhat darker, but still the moonlight came in great splashes through the trees. By the advantage of this unequal gleam, Ruggles caught sight of a man approaching—a man in evening dress, bareheaded and smoking a pipe.

It was William, who had also his emotions and uneasinesses, and felt the need of the cool of the night.

No sooner did Stephen recognize the face than he threw aside his romance like a costume of masquerade and determined to come down to business on the spot. He stood still in the road and waited till the other came up.

"Good evening," he said. "Are you taking the air?"

"Might as well do that as anything else," replied William, with a touch of hostility. "There's nothing going on up at ours."

"Then if you are not in a hurry, we might have a talk for a few minutes. I have a question to ask you."

"If it's about poetry," said William, "I *am* in a hurry." And he made as if to pass on.

The other laid a hand on his sleeve. "It is not about poetry. Not just now, at least. It is about something which you can account for more easily. The question may seem abrupt—but would you mind telling me just where you stand with Miss Hazard?"

William's ruddy face turned as pale as the very moon. "He's a lawyer, and she's instructed him to go for me." Such was his thought, and it was sufficiently nerve-shaking. But if he weakened now he was lost, and he squared himself as well as he could for the onset.

"I don't know what right you have to interfere," he brought out morosely. "What are you mixing in for?"

To Ruggles, William's lack of surprise in front of the question was in itself a luculent proof that close relations with Pen had prevailed at some time or other; and his heart was sore. Still, that could not be helped; and if it could, it did not matter now.

"My right," he answered frigidly, "is quite simple to explain. I am going to marry Miss Hazard."

William leaped back with such force that he banged against a tree. "You!" he shouted in the night. "O my God! You!"

The relief from the tension, the dread, of the late miserable hours was so sudden, this lifting of the fog of his difficulties so sweet, that he almost broke down and cried. He began to laugh instead.

Ruggles strode up to him. "If you don't drop that," he said, "I'll smash you."

William waved his hand feebly. "No, no!" he expostulated incoherently. "It's not anything like that. Give you my word it ain't. No offence meant, and that kind of thing. But—but—look here; I'm engaged too. I may as well tell you. I'm engaged to Sabina Moll."

Ruggles received this with the famous equanimity he used to show in court when a surprise was sprung on him by the other side. But he looked at it carefully, and wondered if he had better ask any more questions. He concluded that as things were shaping it would be more for his own dignity and that of his future wife to let the matter die then and there. This engagement to Sabina put Spring out of action as a practical agent. And he would hear what Penelope had to say to-morrow.

So he congratulated William. The youth was mopping his linen cheeks and brow, still under the influence of the shock.

"No doubt you will live in Manchester?" said Ruggles, for the sake of saying something.

"Yes—no," William gulped. "That is—I mean, there's nothing settled yet. Whew! I suppose that bar at the hotel would be closed now. I'm not very strong sometimes. I feel the need of a little refreshment."

"They'll give you what you want," said Ruggles, who missed nothing of the young man's consternation, "if you explain who you are. Mention your uncle's name. It must be the weather."

"Just so." William fanned himself with his handkerchief. "The weather—sudden change—oh Lord!"

They stood chatting a few minutes longer on indifferent subjects: the weather, the state of the roads, the latest cricket. Had William managed to see a London newspaper? No. He had heard about the war? "Oh, yes," said William, thinking of Sabina that afternoon.

For the first time in their acquaintance the barbed wire was stripped off. There was no more antagonism in their bearing; there was even that cordiality such as springs up between two people bent on the same enterprise. They were just two wayfarers on the perilous road of life, mindful of sympathy, grateful for a word of cheer.

Their looks were kind and friendly; their looks had something of the encouragement and pathos plain in the looks given to men who are embarking on a risky voyage. At parting they gripped hands. Neither envied the other.

"I hope she loves him well enough to forgive the poetry, if ever she finds it out," Ruggles thought.

And William was thinking: "I hope he'll be able to manage Pen."

They really felt very kindly to one another. So much so, that when they had gone a little way each felt the need to look at the other's receding back. William turned round and found that Ruggles was looking after him.

To cover their confusion, they waved at each other vaguely.

Chapter XXVI

ALTHOUGH IT WAS JUST on eleven, the hour when the bar of the hotel closed to those who were not staying in the house, the landlady, who recognized William, obligingly gave him a drink. She was a pleasant, talkative woman who carried much finery; and as William found his drink too long and strong to gulp down at once, she chatted with him as he stood there. He was still too agitated to pay much heed to what she said. She seemed to be talking about war.

"An officer from Southampton who was here for dinner this evening said he was sure we'd be in it. Do you think we shall, Mr. Spring?"

William had formed no opinion whatever about the matter, his own policy during the last few weeks requiring all the attention he had to spare.

"Not a chance," he said at random.

"Well, now, that's what *I* say. We're not going to fight about Servia—not likely. We have a good many Germans in here off and on in the summer-season. Come over from the Island, y'know. Of course they're not English gentlemen and ladies; but I like them better than the French and Americans myself. Good night, sir. Thank you."

When he reached "The Firs," he found his uncle, who had just got in from the Isle of Wight, standing near a lamp in the hall, reading aloud from a newspaper to Aunt Laura, Sabina, and Alicia Ford.

"Gratters, my boy," said Uncle Herbert in an absent-minded way, holding out his hand sideways and keeping his eyes on the paper. "Well, it is certainly a rum go."

William's assurance had increased considerably since his interview with Ruggles. He now felt sure of his ground. "I don't see why you should say that," he answered in rather an offended tone. "I think it's quite natural."

Uncle Herbert looked up quickly. "It's quite——? Oh, Lord bless me, I don't mean your engagement, my dear boy! Warmest congratulations. I meant the war."

"We are going to war with Germany," explained Alicia Ford.

"Oh, Alicia, how belligerent you are!" cried Aunt Laura. "Nobody knows."

"I'll be jolly glad," said William. "What is it about?"

"You'll be able to write *such* an extraordinary poem," laughed his aunt. Now that the engagement was quite settled she was becoming a little reckless.

"They were all saying at the yacht-club that we're bound to get into it," pursued Uncle Herbert. "I can't say I'm sorry. It is bound to come some time, if it doesn't now. The Germans are getting too uppish; they need a good thrashing. I never could bear Germans."

"We shall be in Berlin in six weeks," decided Alicia. "They can't make any stand against us. And look at our navy!"

"One Englishman is worth six Germans any day," said William. "You've only to look at them."

"Well, I don't know so much about that," Aunt Laura demurred. "There was a German gentleman I met the other day over at Ringwood—I forget his impossible name—and he was saying that he hoped there wouldn't ever be war with us, but that if there was, England would need no end of help to stand against Germany."

"Oh, that's just their dam' brag, my dear," exclaimed Uncle Herbert. "We'll all be where we are now this time next year talking about the way the Germans were licked."

"Perhaps——" said Aunt Laura.

Alicia spun round at her. "For shame, you, awful woman! I believe you are really horribly unpatriotic. There was an article in one of the Sunday papers yesterday just about people like you."

"Like me? Then I'm sure it was interesting, Alicia dear."

"Of course *I'll* go to the front," declared William. There was some importance in his voice.

"That's right, my boy. I only wish I was your age," approved his uncle.

"But wouldn't there be some training or something necessary?" hesitated Alicia.

"Oh Lord, no!" said William. "Anybody of decent age who can shoulder a rifle."

Sabina glided forward, blushing very prettily. "Oh, please don't!" she murmured.

It was as if she had fallen on his breast dramatically and cried out "My Hero!" The three women gazed at William with tender eyes, and he felt some of the charm which the warrior in all ages has derived from the applause of women.

Then, without thinking much what he was saying, he added:

"Mother would never look at me again if I didn't go."

They all realized that there at last was a definite and sincere word. They called to mind the straight-standing, rapid-speaking, high-hearted woman, sprung from generations of soldiers, representing the British Army caste, and the widow of a soldier; and they knew well that if there was a call for her son, she would disown him if he faltered. ...

So deeply did they feel this that nobody spoke for a little. Then Uncle Herbert, knowing well that the moment war was declared, William would have to go, took the young man by the hand.

"My dear lad," he said awkwardly.

Sabina broke down in tears.

❧

About the same hour, Pen, lying awake, heard Mrs. Wrench coming upstairs, and opened her door to ask if she might have her bath a half-an-hour earlier in the morning.

"I've been sitting up till Mr. Wrench came home," said Mrs. Wrench. "He's been up to London on the cheap excursion to the Crystal Palace. He says all the talk is that we're going into war."

Pen hardly ever glanced at a newspaper. "What war?" she asked dreamily, looking at Mrs. Wrench through her hair which rolled in waves over her face and shoulders down to her waist. The candle Mrs. Wrench held threw the light upon the girl's face on which an unconscious rapture lingered.

"How nice you look, miss," said Mrs. Wrench involuntarily. "It's a war with the Jarmints. I'm sure I don't know myself what they want to be fighting for. First it was the Suffragettes, and now it's the Jarmints. Do you think they'll ever get over here?"

Although Pen was quite unable to estimate the shock which was beginning to make the earth tremble, she could judge its gravity far better than the people at "The Firs." "I don't think it is altogether unlikely," she answered.

"Mr. Wrench was saying he wished we had somebody else standing by us instead of the French. He never had a mind for the French. I can't say as I object to the Jarmints myself. I had one of them here last year, the Baroness—well, I fair forget her name—a friend of her Ladyship's up at the Court. She was as nice a lady as you want to see, and gave no trouble. But Lord bless you, miss, they're all foreigners, however you look at them. Let the foreigners fight it out between 'em, I say."

Pen came to the one point where her thoughts centred. "If war does come, Mrs. Wrench—you know, if men are called up in addition to the regulars, do you think Mr. Ruggles would go?"

"Oh yes, indeed, he would," said Mrs. Wrench immediately. "He'd be one of the first. Why, he's always gone on so much about the Territorials—he goes into camp with them every year. When Lord Roberts was in the town to make a speech last November, Mr. Ruggles took the chair at the meeting. I went to it with my niece, but nobody thought of war then. We were wondering what the Suffragettes would do."

"Well, there's one thing," Mrs. Wrench added. "It won't be as long as the Boer war. It's not so far for our men to go, you see. Good night, miss."

Penelope sat up in bed, with her lithe hands clasped about her knees. Yes; she was sure he would go to the war. He might be killed. She was far too much of an everyday heroine not to look at that. If he married her before he went away, and then was killed, she would be his widow; perhaps mistress of half of Palebrook; at any rate, secure and enviable for life.

With that she felt for the first time that she was really in love with him. It was not imagination or caprice or flirting this time; neither was it the desire to make a lucky marriage. He had come to bring her happiness because he saw she was unhappy and solitary. Nobody else had done that. She could never bear to lose him now.

She had lived entirely for herself hitherto: at this moment a new life was opening, full of pain, full of splendour too. Suddenly, without any preparation, she had a revelation of the unity of the universe, and saw that the smallest affairs of the most insignificant men and women are affected by the general anguish and convulsion of humanity.

She was content now to abide by life as it was, since into her heart had come what she prized above life, what made her one with the acquiescence and quiet of the trees and grass. She would not marry him till he came back. She would return to London and keep on giving lessons till the war ended and he was home again. That was the best thing to do. Then, if he were killed, she would have no comfort which he would have given her and could not share.

She sat on the side of the bed, thinking, till the early summer dawn bleached the window-panes. She got up and opened the window. It was a sullen dawn without promise of sun.

And as she gazed into the greyness, she had a dim premonitory vision of what she did see about two months later, when she stood on the platform of Charing-Cross station watching a khaki-clad arm still waving to her from a disappearing train, and thought that nothing— nothing in the world mattered now if he did not come back.

THE END

www.ingramcontent.com/pod-product-compliance
Lightning Source LLC
Chambersburg PA
CBHW061249170626
46809CB00007B/2921